DIRTY TRICKS

JOHNS HOPKINS: POETRY AND FICTION
John T. Irwin, General Editor

Fiction Titles in the Series

DIRTY TRICKS

SHORT STORIES BY
JACK MATTHEWS

THE JOHNS HOPKINS UNIVERSITY PRESS
Baltimore and London

The Johns Hopkins University Press, 701 West 40th Street,
Baltimore, Maryland 21211
The Johns Hopkins Press Ltd., London

I would like to express my appreciation to the editors of the following publications, where all but two of these stories were published: *Balcones Review, Best American Short Stories 1977, Black Ice, Gamut, Kenyon Review, Malahat Review, Mississippi Valley Review, Onionhead, Southern California Anthology, Southern Review,* and *Western Humanities Review.*

I would also like to give special thanks to the Ohio Arts Council for a Major Artist's Grant in 1989–90.

Library of Congress Cataloging-in-Publication Data

Matthews, Jack.
    Dirty tricks : short stories / by Jack Matthews.
        p.   cm.—(Johns Hopkins, poetry and fiction)
    ISBN 0-8018-4053-8 (alk. paper)
    ISBN 0-8018-4054-6 (pbk.)
    I. Title.   II. Series.
    PS3563.A85M3   1990   90-30832
813'.54—dc20   CIP

CONTENTS

DIRTY TRICKS

FUNERAL PLOTS

Sitting on the patio after dinner, Walt Thatcher sensed that his wife was preoccupied. The two of them hadn't spoken for perhaps five or ten minutes, although it was becoming increasingly difficult for him to estimate time accurately. Still it must have been something like that. Perhaps fifteen minutes, but surely no more. It was late summer, and the cricket songs were pleasantly loud and rhythmic, emanating from the hedges at the rear of their two-acre lawn and in the thick under-growth beyond.

Walt could also hear music from somewhere inside the house, although he couldn't identify the composer. Mid-nineteenth-century, perhaps; maybe Schumann, maybe Brahms. It was a piano concerto, he thought; but couldn't be sure. His memory had begun to do odd things to him since his stroke several months ago. A year? No, he didn't think that long, but it had been some time. Months and months. *Several* months, whatever that might be.

Often they were quiet after dinner, and he thought of this quietude as a kind of beautiful peacefulness, knowing even as he thought so that for Doris it might be the most terrible sort of boredom. Why did he brood so much these days over how she felt? There had been a time when he could have felt assured of their essential sympathy, a time when she'd enjoyed their silence together as much as he. Only, lately, he sensed that the character of her share in that silence had changed. And yet, to take the long view, hadn't their ten or fifteen years of marriage proved warm and satisfying?

Because it hadn't been built upon the typical infatuation of a man facing his middle-age crisis . . . it wasn't as if Walt Thatcher, at the age of sixty, had married a twenty-five year old. Doris had been a mature, divorced woman of, what, forty, at least. Maybe forty-five. Only the other evening he had asked her, and she had answered— surprised that he could have forgotten—but she had answered, anyway. Still, the answer she had given had gone gulping down the drain of forgetfulness, like so much.

This evening they were sitting on opposite sides of the table, each in a wheeled padded lawnchair that rolled easily on the flagstones. She was looking at a catalog advertising women's clothing, and he was simply sitting there, letting his thoughts drift, vaporous as veils of rain in the distant sky.

The evening air continued warm from the heat of afternoon, but the lengthening shadows loomed darker against the bright minty green of the well-tended lawn at the far edge; and he sat there comfortable, wondering if Doris had been forty or forty-five when they'd gotten married all those years before, he couldn't remember exactly how many. But whatever that mystic number was, she was still a handsome woman of middle age—sixty-something, but beautifully groomed and with a cheerful countenance and a good, firm figure.

So this, he heard himself recite somewhere inside his head, was old age. "But then, thou must outlive thy youth, thy usefulness. . . ." Proud that he could remember Milton, he tried to remember the rest . . . but it wouldn't come. A stanza that ended, "fall, like ripe fruit, into thy mother's lap," anyway. The mother being earth, of course; a most uxorious—or at least, female-loving—image for Milton, who was supposed to have been something of a misogynist.

A soft breeze came over him, bristling the hairs on his arms, and the old lines of poetry sifted out of his mind. Perhaps it was better this way, he often reminded himself, and remembered doing so; for when you die at an advanced age, there is not so great a loss, since so much of what you were has already departed through the small, silent attritions of the years.

"I was wondering," she said.

He lifted his face and looked at her. "What?"

"You weren't listening."

"Sorry. I didn't hear you."

She nodded and carefully laid the catalog on the table between them. "Not surprised," she said.

He had not heard the first of that, but he knew what she must have said, and nodded.

"Walt, I have something to show you."

Something in the way she said it, something in her expression, alerted him. What had she been leading up to? Surely, she had been chatting about something, for there was an odd and disconcerting air of conclusiveness in the way she'd said it.

"I said," she said slowly, "I have something to show you."

"Like what?" he asked.

"Something you should look at. And think very seriously about."

"Well, I would assume that."

"Would you really?" she asked, tilting her head and smiling at him. It was a very small smile, and in some way not entirely humorous. There was something almost old and tired in it; it occurred to him that it was an expression he could not at the moment remember having ever seen in her face.

"Well, let's see it, then," he said gruffly. "Bring it out, whatever it is. Another new dress? Some extravagance you haven't told me about, Doris?"

She shook her head no. "No, you'll have to come inside. It's something you should look at inside."

He thought about that a moment, then nodded. "All right, if you want to be mysterious. We'll see if the old legs will get me out of this damned thing."

"And don't forget your cane."

He looked at her. "Of course I won't forget the cane. How could I? The first step or two would remind me."

He pulled himself to an upright seated position, swinging his legs to the side so that his feet rested on the sturdy aluminum edge of the lawn chair and eased his weight onto his legs and finally lifted himself to his feet. Then he leaned over and picked up the cane that had been slanted, notched between the arm and the chair.

"All right," he said. "I'm ready. Where are we off to?"

"The bedroom."

Walt nodded. "Ah, the bedroom! She's going to try to see if she can get a rise out of the old gentleman, after all these years."

She laughed distantly. "Oh, no: nothing like that, I'm afraid."

"Why 'afraid'?"

"Oh, I don't know. You figure it out. You've always been good at figuring things out, haven't you?"

He paused after one step. "I'm not sure I want to answer such a question when you ask it like that."

She motioned to him, wiggling her index finger. "Come on, come on. There's nothing to be afraid of, after all."

3

"What do you mean, 'after all'?"

"Just come along like a good boy, will you?"

"I'm not a boy—good, bad, or indifferent. I am an old man, which I would guess means indifferent."

"Really? I'm sure I hadn't noticed."

He stepped carefully over the threshold of the sliding doors and said, "What in the hell's gotten into you, Doris?"

"Not a thing. Just come along. We have something very important to discuss. Even critical, you might say."

Saying that, she walked at a sprightly pace into the bedroom, and he followed, plodding forward with his cane and favoring the numbness in his left leg. "It'd better be important," he grumbled.

"Oh, you'll see that it is."

He was a little surprised that she'd heard, but that was all right. And by the time he reached the open door of their bedroom, he was feeling downright curious. It wasn't like Doris to play games, so he reasoned that this game must have a very special significance.

But his brief surmise did nothing to prepare him for what faced him when he entered the bedroom, for he saw that she had hung two of his favorite old suits side by side on hangers from the door of their big, walk-in closet. One suit was black, and the other was a very dark gray. Both a bit old-fashioned, but representing the very best English tailoring and made of one hundred percent wool, of course. The dark gray had been the suit he'd worn, oh, ten or twenty years ago, when he'd represented the Rawlings Corporation in a local property dispute, shortly before he'd retired.

"Why do you have those two suits hanging there?" he asked.

For a moment, she didn't answer. She had her back toward him, and she stepped forward and caressed the sleeve of one of them, as if the arm of the man he'd once been might still be inside.

"All right, I give up," he said. "What's this all about?"

She turned back to him, and, smiling, asked, "All right, which one would you like to be buried in?"

For a moment his mouth got dry and he couldn't have spoken if he'd wanted to. Then, gradually, he eased himself over to the upholstered chair in the corner and sat down. "I see," he said finally.

"After all, it's something I should know," she said practically. "Things being what they are."

"I see," he muttered.

"You *do* see, don't you?"

Gazing at her, he saw her entire body ripple, as if she were no more than a reflection in water that had been mildly agitated by a dropped pebble. He took a deep breath and said, "You know very well that all of this was decided long ago, Doris. We agreed on everything when we were married."

"Two innocent lambs we were, weren't we?" she said, smiling still harder. "How well I, for one, remember. You a widower, and I a divorcée. You were the lucky one, though; better to have a mate die than have him leave you."

"I don't suppose you have the authority to say that unless you've experienced both."

"Well, no doubt I will before long."

"My God!"

"Let's not be maudlin, shall we?" I asked you a very simple question that requires a very simple answer: "which suit would you like to be buried in?"

"You know perfectly well the answer to that: neither one."

"Come, come, Walt: we can't be shown in the casket in our birthday suit, can we?"

"What in the hell has gotten into you, Doris? I've told you a hundred times I don't want any *viewing*, as they call it. I don't want to be embalmed, even. But even if that's the state law, I still want to be cremated. Right away. I never could tolerate the thought of those barbaric rituals. *Never!* I've always felt that way, and you know it. Even Rita knew how I felt about such things."

"Well, isn't it a shame that poor perfect Rita had to die and leave you to little old me."

"Don't be such a bitch, Doris."

"Oh, it comes easy, if the stakes are high enough. And if you hear the name of Rita often enough. As I have through the years, God knows!"

"What are you talking about? I hardly ever mention Rita's name."

"Oh, *don't* you, now! Why, it's 'Rita this, and Rita that, and Rita kiss my nose'!"

"Doris, where in the hell did you get such nonsense? Have you been drinking too much already?"

"Only the honest truth. And the sound of Rita's name ringing like a bell for more than two decades would have driven most wives away . . . but, as you see, I've stuck it out. And will continue to stick it out to the bittersweet end."

He shook his head and pushed down on his cane, trying to lift himself out of the chair. "I don't know what you're talking about, Doris!"

"Oh, I think you do. Your memory is bad, all right; but it's not *that* bad!"

"Well, tell me, then. Come right on out with it, if you've got something to say."

This time he did manage to lift himself shakily to his feet, and, step by step, leaning heavily on his cane and clearing his throat so he wouldn't hear her, he began to work his way out of the bedroom. He had gotten halfway down the hall when he heard Doris walk up behind him. "Don't you walk away from me when I have something to tell you!" she hissed.

"I'm going back to the patio. It's cooler out there."

"We can turn the air conditioner on."

"No, I like fresh air. Especially at this time of evening."

"Listen, you're going to be awfully sorry if you don't listen!"

"Just leave me alone, for God's sake! I don't want to hear any more."

He opened the sliding screen door and moved slowly out onto the patio, feeling slightly vertiginous, as if he had stepped onto the deck of a ship rolling in a slow swell.

When he had seated himself, he looked up and saw her sitting in her own chair, gazing at him. The top button of her white blouse was hanging by a thread, and in view of her compulsive neatness this suggested a shocking, even sinister, neglect.

"I want to be cremated," he said. "No ifs, ands, or buts. Any other option is abhorrent to me. Question closed. It's in my will."

Doris spread her fingers of her right hand and studied her nails. "Let me put it to you clearly: by the time they read the will, my dear, there will have been a viewing, and you'll be wearing one of those two suits. I can see nothing more reasonable than asking which suit you prefer for the occasion."

He stared at her a moment without speaking. Finally, he inhaled and said, "You know that would be foolish. When the will is read and they find out that you didn't abide by my instructions, you'll forfeit everything I've provided for you."

"Everything you've provided for me!" she whispered contemptuously, glaring at him. "This house and an executrix fee and, what, five hundred dollars a month for as long as I live?"

"Plus the furniture, don't forget. And five hundred dollars should be ample, considering the income from your own investments."

"Why, it's only a token, and you know it."

He nodded. "Yes, it is only a token. But according to our agreement when we were married, we weren't going to mix our estates. We agreed that it would be unfair to our children if we did so."

She smiled slightly. "Walt, I'm impressed by how much you seem to be able to remember when the issue is money . . . *especially* when the issue is money that *I* might inherit!"

"I do have my lucid moments."

"I suspect it has to do with how important the issue is. But you seem to rise to the occasion."

"What is it you want, Doris?"

She closed her eyes a moment, then opened them. "When you changed your will two years ago, I was led to understand that you intended to change it to my benefit."

"And so I did. The house, the conventional executrix fee—which is only fair, I don't mind saying—and the monthly stipend."

"Five hundred dollars a month won't even keep me in clothes."

"Then perhaps you'll change your spending habits. Perhaps you'll draw on some of your own income, which is getting fatter all the time. I see nothing unreasonable in that."

"What is unreasonable," she said carefully, slowly, feeling her way with the words, "is that I have four grown children—all with families of their own, along with the natural expenses of raising them and sending them to college—and you have only two grown children, one not even married."

"There's no reason to bring that up now."

"There's every reason to bring it up now. Four is twice as many as two, in case you've forgotten your arithmetic."

"Doris, don't be so goddamn insulting. My memory may be faulty, but my reasoning powers are not all that diminished. What's your point, anyway?"

"My point is that, whatever so-called 'agreement' you may think you remember about our marriage . . . whatever the terms that may or may not have been part of this so-called agreement, they were never put in writing; and the fact is, I don't remember it at all as you state the matter. All I can remember is one evening we talked about how 'it would be nice if we could keep our estates apart'—it was all very hypothetical and theoretical, as I remember it. And whose memory do you suppose will be judged more reliable, yours or mine?"

"In this case, mine. I remember very clearly."

"Well, as efficient as you were then—and such a brilliant and distinguished attorney, I'll remind you—why wouldn't you have had

7

it down in black and white? After all, the way you're referring to it, it was nothing more than a verbal contract . . . and as you've told me many times, a verbal contract is no contract at all."

"I've always insisted upon the term 'oral contract' to distinguish it from a written contract, because in one sense *all* contracts are verbal."

"I stand corrected."

"You will never stand corrected, Doris; I'm afraid you are simply, hopelessly incorrigible."

"Well, we'll see. Or, *I'll see.* Because we're losing sight of the present issue, which is which suit you choose to be wearing at the viewing."

"You really are a disgusting bitch, aren't you?"

"I knew you'd get around to saying that, and it doesn't really bother me. But for your information, no, I am not; I merely have my own priorities as a mother, as well as a woman who has a certain amount of personal pride and resents the humiliation of your settlement. If you'd really done something worthwhile when you changed your will two years ago, this question wouldn't even be coming up now, and those two suits would not be hanging from the door. So what's it to be?"

"You know I can't bear the thought of having my corpse filled with formaldehyde or whatever they use and then having it stuffed inside a coffin."

"The way I see it, there's only one fair solution: slice your estate right down the middle. Not only would that be simple justice, it would be a very small price to pay, considering all I've done for you during the past twenty-two years . . . how I've nursed you and taken care of you. Not to mention what I've had to put up with; how I've kept silent all this time; how I've kowtowed to your every whim and notion."

"You sound as if you came to me in rags and I kept you that way. You were far from being poor, you know. And you're even more comfortable now, because you've been living off me. Nothing wrong with that, but it's allowed your own estate to grow in ways it couldn't have grown otherwise."

"No, I wasn't poor. And I admit I'm not poor now. But I can feel the financial burden of my children—I wouldn't be a decent mother if I didn't; and considering the way I've had to take care of you all this time, it isn't fair that *your* two should receive more than my four, especially when mine need money far, far more than yours."

"Rick doesn't."

She nodded. "No, that's true. Rick is doing very well, and I'm proud of him. But what about the others? They're all struggling in debt, to some degree or other."

"Letty and Ron are trying to live beyond their means, that's what *their* problem is."

"Oh, yes? Well, just tell me this, Walt: who's to decide what's beyond their means? You?"

"No, the fiscal realities of the world they live in. It's relative, of course; but the test is, are they happy or not? And if they're not living at the starvation level—which I'll remind you they most emphatically are *not*—then the trouble's not in their income, but in how they handle it . . . and how greedy they are for more."

She made a face. "Don't talk to me of greed and fiscal realities. I've had to listen to too many of your lectures, and I'm not about to tolerate another."

"Actually, I've never understood why you haven't filtered some of your own dividends off to them, if you're so worried about them. You've got plenty to spare."

"I've got my old age to think of, don't forget. You're practically past all that; you're almost safe at home, you might say; but I might have twenty or thirty years left. And what if something should happen to me? I don't ever, ever want to become a burden."

"You're already a burden."

"Well, aren't we witty this evening."

"Fifty-fifty, you say?"

"I ask you, what could be more fair?"

"Now let me get this straight: if I don't change my will, you'll have my body embalmed and put in a goddamn casket so it can be 'viewed' by friends and relatives and enemies and any passing ghoulish types who might have developed a fondness for such ceremonies?"

"I'll promise it will be a very, very handsome and expensive casket, along with a fine headstone, if you wish. I'll even see that it bears a favorite inscription of yours, if you want. Something from Milton, perhaps? You used to quote Milton a great deal, as I remember."

"My will already specifies that I choose to be cremated . . . and you're right, I suppose: if it's important enough for you to forfeit what I've left to you, then you could go ahead and have my body embalmed and laid out in a casket. But what if I call my lawyer and make a specific point of having my wishes followed?"

"I assume you're talking about Pete, who drew up your last will. Well, Pete's a good old boy, and no doubt as obedient as hell . . . but stop and think a minute. Who's going to be with you when you croak?

Me, that's who. Your loving and faithful wife. And I'll have you embalmed and in your suit before Pete even knows you're dead. And if he asks me, what do you suppose I'll say? Why, I'll say that you told me you'd changed your mind and had talked about getting back to him so that he could put your most recent wishes in a codicil; because you wanted to be buried like everybody else, including your old momma and daddy, whose bodies are still rotting away in their caskets, the way God meant for them to rot away."

"Stop it, will you?"

"No, I won't. And as a matter of fact, I could even go in the opposite direction and say you were so crazy two years ago that you couldn't have made a sane decision. Even if they don't agree with me, what do you think they'd do? You say I'd forfeit my inheritance, such as it is: I say that's nonsense—I'd take it to court, and win, and pay the expenses out of the estate. Because no *sane* man gives a damn about what happens to his body after he's dead, because everybody knows it doesn't matter. And do you think they're going to take a widow to court over such a sad and silly business as that?"

For a long moment he was silent. Finally he said, "Well, you've learned something from living with me, I'll say that."

"*I'll* say I have!"

He shook his head solemnly. "To think it would come to this; to think you would ever blackmail me like this."

"Actually," she said, "it would be more accurate to call it extortion, if you'll excuse my correcting a man who was once said to have such a fine legal mind."

"That's right, extortion."

"But I'd say a more proper term yet is simple justice."

"You probably would," he said, and closed his eyes as he took a deep breath and exhaled.

"So what's it to be? Do I phone Pete and ask him to come over so that you can make a new will? Or do you choose which suit you want to wear in your casket? Or do you want me to choose your suit for you? It wouldn't be the first time . . . although it would certainly be the last."

For a moment he was silent. It was getting dark out, and the crickets were louder than ever. "All right," he said. "Call Pete."

She nodded. "Good. I'll call him right now, at home. Maybe he can come tomorrow. Considering who it is, he'll drop everything else. I'll stress how urgent you feel it is that you make a new will right away. You do agree that you feel urgent about it, don't you?"

"Yes," he said, "I guess I do, under the circumstances."

10

"Actually, I think what I'm asking is very modest. And it's not as if *your* two need money, is it?"

"No," he said, "they're doing pretty well. And as for you, you're a model of temperance."

She laughed and told him how pleased she was that he understood and was willing to be realistic about the whole thing.

Then she went inside and phoned their attorney, Pete Schreiber, who agreed to come to their house on the afternoon of the next day with all the necessary legal forms. Pete itemized these, emphasizing the complexity of the transaction because of the size of the estate; but Doris hardly listened.

When he finished, however, she thanked him, said good-bye, and returned to the patio, where she informed her husband that all would be taken care of the next day. "Now whatever you do," she said, laughing, "don't die tonight just to frustrate me."

"I'll do what I can, Doris," he said.

"And when it all works out the way it should be, I'll promise that you'll be cremated and your ashes scattered over the flower borders, just as you wanted it."

"So you do remember."

"Why, of course I remember," she said. "Every single word."

It was almost three-thirty the next afternoon when Pete Schreiber arrived. Although he himself was no older than Doris, his firm had been formed by two lawyers from Walt Thatcher's own law office shortly after Walt's retirement, and Walt had retained a close and cordial personal relationship with the younger firm.

Pete rang the bell, and the Thatcher's maid, Imogene, admitted him and let him go back to the family room at the rear, where Walt and Doris were waiting. Pete was a large, bald man with a large, shapeless nose and a drooping ginger mustache. He was the son of Tom Schreiber, who had been one of the founders and senior partners of the branch firm; only Tom was partially retired, and Pete took care of most of his business. This afternoon, Pete was wearing a light tan open-necked shirt that showed a cluster of red hair at the top of his chest. He wore a diamond ring on each hand and a solid gold Riscotti handmade watch on his left wrist.

Doris greeted him and asked if he wanted a drink, which Pete declined, saying it was a bit early for him, but please go ahead if they liked.

"We do like," Doris said in a festive voice, picking up a Bloody

11

Mary and holding it high for him to see, "and we have already taken your advice. Pre-facto, if that's a word. If not, well, pre-facto anyway."

Grinning, Pete turned to Walt and said, "Well, Doris is in rare good humor today, I see; and it looks like the party's begun. And how are you doing?"

"I've been worse," Walt said in a faraway voice.

"Well, glad to hear that, anyway. What's this business about changing your will again?"

For a long moment Walt merely stared out at nothing.

"Walt?" Doris said.

He lifted his head, and she said, "Surely, you heard what Pete asked you just now. Why didn't you answer?"

Walt stared at Doris a moment and then turned to Pete. "Hello, Pete," he said.

Pete laughed nervously. "Hey, I just came in and we all greeted one another. And Doris asked me if I wanted a drink. Remember? You probably didn't recognize me because I said no."

"Why are you here, Pete?"

Glancing quickly at Doris, Pete turned back to the old man, who was leaning slightly to the side as he sat in his chair. "Hey, are you all right?" he asked.

"Of course I'm all right. What is it you want?"

Doris said, "His hearing isn't all that good." Then in a loud, angry voice, she said, "Listen, Walt, I called Pete last night and asked him to come on over because you wanted to change the will. Surely, you remember."

Vaguely, Walt nodded.

When he didn't say anything, Pete said, "So you want to change your will again. Is that right, Walt?"

"Yes," Walt said. "Rita wants me to change the will."

"Who?"

"What in the hell are you talking about?" Doris yelled.

"Who's Rita?" Pete asked. "Wasn't that his . . . "

"You know damned well who it was," Doris whispered. "And so does *he*! Rita was his first wife, and she died thirty years ago."

Pete shook his head. "Hey, maybe we'd better put this off for the time being."

"The time being, *shit!* He knows goddamn well who I am, and I'm not about to be taken in by his sick little games!"

"Sick is the word," Pete said in a low voice.

"No, I didn't mean it that way," Doris said. "He's just trying to get even with me."

"Get even with you for what?"

Doris blinked and thought a moment. "I don't like to talk about it."

"Well, if you don't talk about it to me, and I'm your lawyer, what do you expect me to do?"

She nodded. "All right. Walt promised me several months ago that he wanted to change his will and divide his estate right down the middle, which is only fair, as anybody could see. Anyway, he said he wasn't comfortable with the will he had you draw up two years ago because it obviously *wasn't* fair—especially considering how much would go to his own children, and how little would come to me, or to mine. Especially after I'd, you know, done so much for him, and everything all these years. Also, as a protection in my old age."

"I see," Pete said.

"You can see how it is," Doris said. "Listen, that old man is as sharp as a tack. His memory may be a little funny now and then, but he hasn't lost an ounce of his intellectual ability, and I'm in a position to know. What he's doing now is just having his little fun. He's been awfully bored lately, and entertained himself with some pretty far-out jokes."

In a louder voice, Pete said, "Is that right, Walt? Do you want to change your will again?"

"Whatever Rita says," the old man muttered, waving his hand at Doris.

For a moment no one spoke. The clock was ticking, and Imogene was making distant noises in the kitchen, preparing dinner.

Doris suddenly got up and went over to him. "Listen, don't think I don't know what you're trying to pull, and don't think you'll get away with it!"

"I think I'd better be going," Pete said in a low voice to her. "I didn't have any idea he was this bad."

"I didn't either," Doris muttered.

"Well, I guess I'd better be going, then."

Doris took him by the arm and led him to the hall entrance. "All right, it's probably best you shouldn't witness any more of his skill as an actor. I'll only point out to you that I am as certain as I am that you're standing there that he's just putting all this on."

"Why on earth would he want to do that?" Pete asked.

Doris shook her head vigorously. "Oh, never mind, Pete. We've all had too many Bloody Marys, that's the problem."

"You mean, Walt's been drinking them, too?"

For a moment she paused, thinking; then she said, "I'm afraid

13

that's only the truth, and this early in the day. As you can see, I joined him. But Imogene took his glass back in the kitchen right before you came. He gets like this when he's been drinking."

Pete shrugged. "Well, whatever, it's no time to make a new will. If I can help, get in touch."

"You'd better believe we'll be in touch," Doris said.

Pete frowned a moment, then patted her on the shoulder and left.

When she went back in to the family room, she said, "Well, I suppose you think you've been awfully goddamn clever, don't you?"

When he didn't answer, she stared at him more closely. "Did you hear what I said?"

"I heard," he said finally.

"And in case you really are slipping your gears, I'm not Rita; she's been dead for thirty years. I'm your wife, Doris."

"I know goddamn well who you are," Walt said.

"And I still have to figure out what suit you'll be wearing, unless you decide to change the will, as you promised."

Walt shook his head and handed her several sheets from his private p.c. printer. "I wouldn't bother, Doris. Maybe you noticed I was busy in my study all morning. Well, here are the fruits of my labor. I suggest you look at it very closely. You will see it's an instrument referring to my wish to be cremated, explaining that, frequently, throughout the term of our marriage, you have been fully informed of my preference for cremation over burial; and if you do not follow my instructions regarding cremation, not only will you be immediately discharged as executrix, but in view of your willful meddling in my long, constant, and undeviating choice to be cremated, you will be sued by the estate. I will remind you that the estate is a legal entity, and will remain so long after my death; it will be a corporation, of sorts; and whoever your successor might be (I suspect it will be Pete himself), he will be legally obligated to sue you. And supposing he himself is corruptible—which I don't think to be so, but believe you will try him, anyway—I have sent copies of this will, along with suitable retainers, to various other agencies which I will not name, but which will have an obligation to see that the intention of my will in this regard is carried out."

When he finished, Doris sat down in an upholstered chair, staring distantly at the remains of her Bloody Mary, which she finally decided to finish. Then she licked her lips and said, "Very clever, but it won't work; Pete can testify that you're bonkers."

"Irrelevant. This instrument, which I intend to execute tomor-

14

row (reminding you that copies have already gone out—Imogene and the maid next door, what's her name, were witnesses and each signed six copies), will simply reinforce what is intrinsic to all of my previous wills, for the clause about cremation is in all of them—a fact to which I give great emphasis, of course. So my present mental state is irrelevant as to substance, but representative of my passionate concern over this matter, and enjoining the estate to seek restitution if cremation is not carried out as I have determined. I might also add that, like Sophocles of old, the character and precision of my prose speak volumes, in a manner of speaking, concerning my mental alertness and perspicacity."

Doris nodded. "You say you're going to have this done tomorrow?"

Walt nodded.

"Well, we'll just see about that, won't we?"

"We will," he said. "But I will remind you that copies have already been mailed, so you haven't a ghost of a chance, Doris. I'll be burned or I'll be damned."

Walt Thatcher not only survived the night and did as he had promised the next day, he lived for just over a year, dying in his sleep late in November with the season's first snowfall. Doris had accepted her defeat rather gracefully and good-humoredly, cautioning herself that whatever happened, she should not do anything so foolish as get sued. Not at *her* age, certainly.

So, immediately after Walt's death, she saw that he was cremated, just as he wished. And at the special services at St. George's Episcopal Church, where they had been accustomed to attending services at Easter and Christmas and were regular supporters of the Mission Fund, Doris proved to be a pleasantly sorrowful but dignified widow.

In spite of all, she had been quite content with how things had gone, and she realized that her memories of her second husband would not remain altogether unpleasant. In fact, they might turn out to be rather cozy. After all, Doris herself was getting old, and she might as well face the fact, although she knew there are almost as many ways of facing facts as there are facts, and she planned to do it in the right way—because she was still an attractive woman, when she dressed up, and had not lost all her ability to charm.

She admitted to herself that Walt had not really been a bad husband, as bad husbands go, although she thought it was something of a shame, and a bit ironic, that most of the lucidity of his last two years should have been concentrated upon foiling her plan to inherit more of his estate. Still, she had accepted the fact and had not tried it again. She had consoled herself with the memory that she had given it a shot, it hadn't worked, so it was best to forget about it and go on living the life she had to live. And even though Walt had spent most of his last year in various states of confusion, Doris tolerated it all very well and took care of him.

After his death, she sold the house and contents for just over $685,000—more than she had dreamed it would bring. She moved to a small, comfortable, rather exclusive condominium in Arizona, set up a trust providing for escrow accounts, along with annual gifts of $9,999 to each of her children, and took care to phone all of them twice a week.

She was quite happy, for she had her health and her independence, along with her eye on several quite eligible old gentlemen in the neighboring condos. She would see what she would see. Time would tell. Meanwhile, memories of her life with Walt would prove to be memories she could live with, which was important for her. And which was certainly more than you could have said about her first husband, that son of a bitch, who'd left her, so young and vulnerable, for another woman.

THE GIRL ON THE FLAGPOLE

Back in the 1930s there was a woman flagpole sitter named Beth Olcheski. She claimed to be "The Only Woman Flag Polack Sitter in the World," and climbed a specially built 65-foot pole on top of a six-story building in Milwaukee to await a sponsor. Her husband, Stanley, was her manager, and stood on the roof at the bottom of the pole, greeting people and talking to them, while Beth sat atop the pole and waved to all those who looked up from the sidewalk, 160 feet below.

She stayed there for forty-eight hours without any tangible results, although on the first day newspaper cameramen had taken photographs of her, and the news stories that day and the next had mentioned her need for a sponsor.

But no sponsor was forthcoming. And exactly forty-eight hours after she had climbed up, a reporter named Paul Higgins stood at the base of the pole and called up to her, asking for permission to climb up and interview her. He said that he had just talked with Stanley, who had said it was okay with him, but he had to get her permission first. He said that Stanley had offered to send up a message by rope, but he'd told him he used to be a singer and had a voice that carried well and could easily be heard from that distance, even with the wind.

"How much do you weigh?" Beth yelled back.

"A hundred and sixty-two in my underwear."

She thought a moment, then told him that was a borderline weight, combined with hers, but to come ahead anyway.

Her husband nodded and strapped a harness on him, so that he could climb. He'd already noticed that Paul was wearing tennis shoes that would grip the metal pole. Now he said, "And whatever you do, for Christ's sake, don't start swinging and don't lean forward toward the pole, which is kind of a natural instinct, since you realize it's the only thing that's keeping you up there in the sky. But it's your weight pulling against the pole is what keeps you up there. Think about it."

Higgins assured him that he understood perfectly. Whereupon, he tugged his snapbrim hat down hard on his head, unbuttoned his vest and suit coat, so they could flap loose and give him some muscle room, and then, very slowly and carefully, hand over hand, and step by step, he climbed all the way to the top.

When he arrived there, he clung to the pole by leaning back in his harness and introduced himself to Beth Olcheski, who did not offer to shake hands with him, although they were close enough to reach. In fact, her left knee and his right shoulder were almost touching.

It was even windier that high up in the air, and he saw that she had dull blonde hair that was cut short, like Amelia Earhart's, and a heart-shaped face with a lot of eye shadow. She was wearing pale blue coveralls and flashy imitation diamond earrings.

From her first comments, she sounded bitter. There was something in her voice that reminded him of a spoiled little girl. She told him she was hungry for a good meal, and would give anything for a good American steak, an Irish potato, a Polish salad, and a glass of Italian red table wine. Then, having said this, she looked at him straight in the eye and said, "And, Mister, I mean *anything!* Do you get my meaning?"

"Got your meaning," Higgins said. Right then he realized he was chewing gum, and had been chewing it hard all the way up the flag pole. He spit it out to the side, and wondered if it might hit Beth's husband Stanley in the eye.

"Do you always wear your hat?" she asked.

"Sure. I'm a newspaper reporter. All newspaper reporters wear hats. I even wear mine to church."

"I'll bet. I can tell you're an altar boy. I know all the signs and can tell you're a regular churchgoer, too!"

"Every seventh year, when the moon's full. Why, I even wear this hat to bed."

"I'd sure like to see something like that."

"Maybe some day you will, Honeybunch. Who can tell what the stars have in store?"

"You certainly do talk sweet, Mister; but I'm a girl who's heard it all before, and can't help wondering if you deliver."

Higgins glanced down at the ground, and then back at Stanley who was standing at the edge of the roof, looking up at them. "Well, probably not up on that platform, I wouldn't," he said.

"I wouldn't expect *that* much of a fellow," she said. "But let me tell you something, there sure are better places than *this* to spend your time."

Higgins wrote that down, and then asked once again for the dimensions of the platform she was on.

"Four and a half feet by three feet," she said.

"Somehow, it looks bigger than that."

"Not if you was up here all the time, it wouldn't."

Higgins nodded and adjusted his hat with his pencil and notebook still in his hand.

"Say," she said, "were you really a singer one time?"

"Several times."

"Don't be so smart. What kind of singer? Were you a professional?"

"I got paid once or twice."

"I'll bet you were a tenor, huh? An Irish tenor."

"All Irishmen are tenors, even when they're baritones and basses."

"I wish you'd stop giving me those wise guy answers!"

"Well, I'm supposed to be interviewing you, remember?"

"Yes, I remember. Only don't bother to ask my age."

"A secret, huh?"

"You'd better believe it, Mister. But go ahead and ask some other questions. Like where I was born and do I have brothers and sisters and stuff like that."

"I don't write about stuff like that. What I do is gather impressions. Like what it's like to be up here at the top of a flagpole with a pretty young woman."

"You come on pretty fast, Mister. Is that your impression?"

"Part of it. But don't worry, this story will be about you, not about me."

"Say, do you want my opinion on politics? How about the CCC or the NRA?"

"Some other time, kiddo."

"So now it's kiddo, is it?"

"I've gotten more material than you think. And you won't be disappointed. You'll come out all right."

"I can hardly wait. Only I wish you had a better picture of me. Stanley has some more pictures to hand out, if you think you can use one."

"We might be able to use one at that."

"That would be swell. I really mean it."

"Well, Mrs. Olcheski, I guess that's about it."

"That's about what?"

"You're a smart dame, aren't you?"

"I ain't used to people who say 'aren't.' "

"I see. Does your husband climb up here to visit you after dark?"

She laughed bitterly. "Not a chance. Would you like to be in on a secret?"

"Sure. I'm a newspaperman, ain't I?"

She laughed. "You did that for me, didn't you? That was cute."

"Glad you liked it. So, what's the scoop?"

"Stanley is deathly afraid of heights."

Higgins nodded. "Check. Hubby afraid of heights."

"I guess that'll be all, huh?"

"Pretty much."

"So this has been another one of them goddamn failures. You know what we was wanting, don't you?"

"Sure. You wanted a sponsor. Just like about everybody else. Only, these are hard times, in case you haven't heard. Flagpole sitters outnumber sponsors by about three to one. Sponsors aren't easy to come by. They're as scarce as honest politicians."

She nodded. "Well, it looks like *you're* doing all right without a sponsor."

"I got the newspaper, don't forget."

"Yeah. I was wondering how that worked."

"It doesn't sound to me like you and Mr. Olcheski are getting along too well."

"*Too well.* Jeez, Mister, I like the way you talk, do you know that?"

"I do what I can to impress the female sector, especially when they're good looking."

"I just bet you do. I would have said, *Too good.*"

"I probably could have figured out what you meant."

"I'll bet you could figure out just about anything, cowboy."

"How's come you called me a cowboy?"

"Because you're wearing a hat, I guess."

"Yeah, but this is just your regular smartass snapbrim hat; it's not a Stetson."

"Well, a girl on top of a flagpole don't always pick up on all the subtleties, if you know what I mean."

"Sure. But let me ask you something. 'Olcheski' is your husband's name, so that makes him Polish. But how about you?"

"Oh, I'm Polish, too, if it makes any difference."

"Not to me, it don't."

"Don't overdo it just for my sake," she said.

"Okay, I won't lay it on too thick."

"Aren't you getting kind of tired hanging there against the harness like that?"

"Not when I'm talking to a girl with your looks."

"Oh, sure! I'll bet you think you could hang there forever."

"No, I'd like to take a couple more steps toward Heaven, if you know what I mean."

"I know what you mean, only I'm Catholic, so I don't exactly appreciate your talking like that."

"My apologies."

"Yeah, your apologies *what?*"

"My apologies right up where the light won't shine, Beth."

"My God, but you're awful!"

"I'm just trying to do my job."

"Doing a job at the top of a flagpole is part of your regular routine, is that it?"

"Well, you could put it that way, Beth."

"You say my name like you've known me for about ten years."

"Make it eleven. And you were nine when we first met."

"You're quick, all right. I'll have to say that for you."

"What was your maiden name?"

She nodded. "Okay. Are you ready for this? It was Walinski."

"Wow! From Walinski to Olchinski! What a leap!"

"Don't get too smart, Mr. Higgins. I know a few things about Irishmen, don't forget."

"How could I forget? I didn't know those things in the first place."

"Say, you're Irish, all right. I could tell it when I saw you climbing toward me up the pole. I could tell by the slant of your hat. The only people I've ever seen who wear a snapbrim like that are Irishmen. And I look down the flagpole, and here comes one climbing up toward me with his hat like that, and his head full of smart ideas."

"Didn't you know? The only way Irishmen can get along in this world is by the slant of their hat and the seat of their pants."

"It's been my observation that Irishmen do all right, if you want to know."

"I'm always glad to hear of it. But the Polacks don't do too bad, either, it seems to me. Take Bronco Nagurski, for example."

"You take him."

"Not to mention Alfred Korzybski."

"Whoever he is."

"He wrote a book called *Science and Sanity*. It's a very important book."

"Sure, and I'll bet you've read it."

"Well, let's say I've looked at the pictures."

"Well, he's Greek to me. Anyway, I've heard of the other one. Bronco Nagurski. But I couldn't care less, because I have one Polack too many, if you want to know the truth."

"A newspaperman always wants to know the truth, Mrs. Olcheski."

"How about not calling me that, okay?"

"Okay. Is Beth all right?"

"It seemed to be okay just a minute ago. And if I didn't mind then, I wouldn't mind now, would I? And since you brought the subject up, why the change?"

"I thought I could feel a little draft."

"Not from me, you didn't. I'm just trying to keep going in this crummy world. Anyway, Beth will do for the time being."

"Like that cute little thing you're sitting on, huh?"

"Huh? Oh, I see what you mean. Say, you're pretty fresh, aren't you?"

"You talk faster when the ground's this far away. Am I right?"

"Maybe."

"I could tell. Do you know how?"

"How?"

"Because you've gotten lonely, being up here all alone, all this time."

"I wouldn't be so lonely if it wasn't, if it weren't, for the fact that we haven't gotten a sponsor yet. I'll tell you something, Mister: it's discouraging for a girl who's trying to do something spectacular."

Higgins pretended to write. "'Something spectacular,' eh? That's got a good sound to it."

"Call me Beth. I like it when you say my name. You don't say it like other people do. Not exactly, anyway."

"Sure, Beth."

"Only, they say, 'Share and share alike.' "

"What does that mean?"

"It means I don't know your first name, Mister Higgins."

"Well, it's Paul."

"Paul Higgins. That doesn't sound like it would fit a fresh type like you."

"My middle name's Timothy, if that helps any."

She nodded. "It helps a little bit. You strike me as being more of a Timothy than a Paul."

"This is beginning to have the sound of a theological disputation."

"Well, we're nearer to Heaven, aren't we?"

"Say, you're pretty sharp yourself."

"Aren't your arms getting tired, Paul?"

"No, I'm all right. Let me ask you another question: are you religious, Beth?"

"Yes, but my husband isn't, he's Catholic. That's a joke."

"A pretty good one, too."

"Are you Catholic? I suppose you are, with a name like Higgins."

"I've heard it said that there have been one or two Catholics in the family tree, somewhere."

"I'll tell you something. I'm glad you climbed up here; but I know you must be getting pretty tired of hanging on like that. Anyway, and this is off the record, I was getting pretty lonely up here myself, where all you can hear is the wind and maybe the pigeons now and then. Sometimes you can hear a car honk."

"I'll honk my horn when I pull away."

"That'll be nice, Paul."

He looked around. "I suppose it does get lonely up here all right."

"They say they have these portable radios that run on batteries now. Have you ever listened to a portable radio?"

"They're not very clear," Higgins said.

"Well, that's nice of you to say so. Anyway, when I asked Stanley about one, he thought I was talking about spaceships to the moon. But what the heck, that's just Stanley; he doesn't try to do anything right. All he does is send up my food and things on that rope. You know, whatever a girl needs in a place like this. Mascara and stuff. Anyway, he doesn't never send me up a note or anything. Stanley doesn't think along those lines."

"Are you also thinking of things like love letters, perhaps? Flowers, maybe?"

"Those would be nice, but we've been married three years, so I don't expect anything like that no more. *Any* more."

"You're very understanding, Beth. I'll bet you'd make some fellow a good wife, do you know that?"

"I know it, but do you? And speaking of which, how about you? Are you married?"

"I was, past tense; but these days, I'm as free as a bird."

"Just don't try to fly, okay?"

"Now that you mention it, I've heard of a case or two where a flagpole sitter has tried to do exactly that: they've tried to fly. You've probably read about them. Some of them go crazy after they've been up in the sky a few days."

"Yes, I've read about them."

"And they were men."

"So what, Mr. Higgins? I don't see how a man can sit on a flagpole any better than a woman can."

"The point is, they went a bit wacky for a couple of seconds and took off like a bird. And a couple of seconds in a place like this is all it takes. They just took off, free as a bird. But with lamentable results, Beth."

"Are you worried about me trying something like that?"

"Well, you do sound a little bit like a girl who's getting to the end of her string."

"Aren't you sweet for worrying about me. But don't waste your time on something like that. I don't like Mother Earth that much. When I go down, I'm going to go down as slow as you do, with my harness and everything, step by step. I'm not unstable, like some of those nuts who climb the pole. Anyway, if you know what you're doing, you get used to it. It gets so it doesn't bother you after a while."

"What doesn't?"

"Oh, you know: being this high up; being this far away from everything. Being up above it all, as Stanley likes to kid me, now and then. That is, when I'm close enough to hear him and recognize his features. He's not bad looking, I'll have to say that for him."

"Every girl's dream, no doubt."

"You don't have to be sarcastic, you know. Stanley is a good-looking man, whether another man would notice or not. But women could tell you that. Supposing you'd ever listen to a woman, which I'm not so sure you're the type."

"I always listen to women."

"Sure. And the pope's a cardshark. But do you know something?"

"What?"

"I'll bet you didn't notice. But look down. Don't stare too long, just take a look. Notice how small everything looks?"

"Sure."

"But did you ever think that what we're looking at is the world where we spend practically all our lives, and the things around us seem so big and important and everything. But being up here gives you a different view of things."

"A different perspective."

"That's exactly right. Being up so high makes cars look like they're about the size of shoes, and people look like little toy soldiers."

"Well, I'll have to hand it to you, Beth."

"Hand what to me?"

"You've got what it takes."

"Who said I didn't?"

"Nobody. I was just making an observation."

"So now, this is an observation tower. Is that it?"

"It'll make a good story, I know that."

"Listen, are you going to give me a break, Paul?"

"You mean, make a good story out of it?"

"Sure. What else can I ask for?"

"Plenty. But to answer your question: sure. I'll make it a good one. And maybe we'll have one of our cameramen come back and get another shot of you."

"Stanley has some nice pictures to hand out. You know, you can't see too much, when you take a picture of me from the rooftop, let alone from the sidewalk. I look just like a dot in the sky. A kite or an airplane, or something."

"Well, if you weren't married, I'd suggest that maybe I could buy you dinner some evening when you climb down."

"Is that a real offer? Or are you just teasing?"

"An Irishman never teases."

"Oh, Lord! An Irishman never does anything *but*."

"So that's your answer?"

"I don't think I quite heard the question."

Paul Higgins grinned and shook his head. "Well, I'd better go down and see what I can do about this."

"Say, you mean that . . . maybe you could find a sponsor?"

"Well, I do know Runninger, who owns the department store. He might go for it. He owes me a favor or two, so maybe something could be worked out."

"I'll tell you something, Paul, if you did something like that, a girl could really be grateful, if you know what I mean."

"Sure, I know what you mean."

"Well, g'bye. And be careful going down. Watch your step, like they say."

"I will. And you be careful staying right there. No flights of fancy, and no fancy flights."

"Are you always like this?"

"No, only when I'm up the pole."

"Up the pole, huh? I've never heard that one."

"Well, now you have, Beth."

"Say, Paul, I've really enjoyed getting to meet you and having a nice conversation."

Higgins nodded again and patted her knee, which was still right next to his shoulder.

Then he began to work his way slowly down the pole. When he was about fifteen feet from the roof, Stanley called out to him, "Must have been some story, eh?"

"We might be able to use it," Higgins said.

"Sure. I can hardly wait."

"Hey, don't be cynical. We didn't do badly when she first went up there, did we?"

"I'm practically ready to retire, I'm so rich."

"Well, I'm not rolling in money either, if it's any comfort."

He removed the harness and gave it to Stanley. "So you don't ever go up there, right?"

"What? Did she tell you that?"

"Something like that. She said you don't like heights."

"There's a lot I don't like, but a man's got to live. Right?"

"I suppose so, now that you mention it."

"Which means there was at least one time I climbed a pole like that."

"Do tell."

"Yeah, and don't act so cocky. How do you think I met her?"

"Oh."

"You better believe it. I think that's the way she likes to be courted, if you get what I mean."

"I get what you mean," Higgins said, writing something down in his notebook, and then lifting his face and taking one last look at her before he left.

She looked dark up there so high, but he could see that she was looking down at him. He could tell, because before he even lifted his hand, she was waving to him, and Stanley was saying, "Our kids are staying with her mother this month, but they always get along okay. But even if they didn't, I don't think it would change anything. I'll tell you something, Mister: you're a newspaperman, and you're always running into strange people, but Beth, there, is something out of this world, because I swear, I don't think she could live very long if she didn't have that pole to look forward to. No sir, that pole is life to her, and don't let her griping fool you for a minute. She gripes a lot, but she don't mean a word of it. When she's up there on the pole, do you know what I think? I think she thinks she's really, truly free. You can put that in your paper, too, if you like. You know, if you can use it; because I'll tell you something, I know what kind of woman she is, and what kind she isn't. And there's nobody else like her on earth. You can put that in, too, if you can use it."

"Sure," Higgins said. "I've got a whole lot I can use."

"And here's a picture she likes pretty well. It shows her on a pole in Des Moines, Iowa, last year."

"Fine," Higgins said, taking the picture. "It looks pretty good."

"And just take a look at that smile on her face. Let me ask you something: is that happiness or is that happiness?"

"If I had three guesses," Higgins said, nodding earnestly at the picture, "I'd say it was happiness."

CRITICAL DECISIONS
OF EARLY YEARS

My first four fights were as a middle-weight: two wins, one loss, one draw. Bertie Gunnerman took me aside after the last one, the draw, and he said, "You're paying too much a price."

"For what?" I asked him. I was leaning on the ropes with my headgear on, breathing heavily, but you could have heard Bertie's rasping tenor through a mattress.

"The weight limit," Bertie said, nodding as if somebody else had suggested it.

Sweat was running down my shoulders, and T. K. Shaw was bobbing up and down behind me, like something on a TV screen that would not turn off.

"Put your sweatshirt on," Bertie said, chewing gum and staring at T. K., who was about eight years over the hill but didn't know anything else, much less anything better.

"You're saying I'm a light heavy?" I asked Bertie.

Bertie stopped chewing his gum and nodded. I almost mentioned that I'd told him this right at the beginning, but I didn't. Maybe I had learned something.

"You wilt," Bertie said, and for an instant, there was a Shakespearean sound to it.

"Like lettuce," I told him, nodding a sort of encouragement.

"Light heavy," Bertie said, "and don't give me none of them heavy-light-heavy or middle-light-heavy jokes, because I have heard them all and find them distinctly not funny."

"Sure," I said.

Bertie had learned to be wary of the way I talked, not to mention my attitude. I didn't quite fit in with the Flamboyants, somehow. He said, "With these kinds of athletes, it's just decoration, like a monogram on the shorts, and I don't pay no attention."

But he made it clear that he suspected there might be substance to some of the things I said, and there might be trouble in that. Once, after I'd sparred a few rounds with T. K., he grabbed the back of my neck and said, "Too many reflections out there in the battle zone. Too much reflection upon life and other things. You grasp my meaning?"

"Sure," I said.

Bertie nodded and adjusted his pre-tied bow tie. "The word I like best from an athlete," he said.

So I repeated it: "Sure," but by this time, Bertie was tightrope walking back through the gym toward the bulletin board, where he kept the records on his boys, including me: one born-again light heavyweight, who would no longer have to pretend to such a quantity of leanness and would not be condemned to wilt from the effects of starvation and too much road work.

They say you don't have to be retarded to be a prizefighter, but it helps. Like most old jokes, this one has its relevance as well as its time.

I would cite Gene Tunney, who read Plato; or Archie Moore, who quoted Shakespeare; or Mickey Walker, who took up painting and did well enough for his canvases to sell.

I'd even told Bertie Gunnerman all this, but Bertie didn't seem interested. His only comment was that Mickey Walker, known as the "Toy Bulldog," had done things in the ring that nobody should be able to do and live; only Mickey lived. It was the other guy who suffered, Bertie said, sounding profound.

As a light heavyweight, I did a little better than I had before. In fact, I fought twelve times—eight, three, and one—but I didn't understand Bertie any better after the last fight than I had the first day I walked into the gym, bobbing up and down on the balls of my feet, the way I figured a good fighter, in the pink of condition, was supposed to walk. Bertie was an enigma, which I mentioned to Phil LaCosta one time, only he thought I meant *iguana*, which wasn't so strange, since Bertie did have sort of a lizard look about the eyes.

Sizing me up that first day, Bertie had figured I was too small for a real light heavy, so he put me in the ring with a black middleweight for a few minutes. I punched him silly, even with the sixteen-ounce gloves, and ended up with blood on my undershorts and Bertie saying, "Kid, you got the strength of a horse."

The black kid didn't seem bothered by the blood coming out of his nose, and later on I wondered if maybe he wasn't a bleeder they'd hired for just this sort of thing. Who'd miss a half-cup of blood? Part of a day's work. But I could hear Bertie saying anybody was strong who could make that poor kid's nose bleed. It was like ringing the bell at a carnival. Bertie knew his machinery, and knew where all the pedals were.

He didn't mind if I went to college; in fact, he seemed to think it might be interesting. He liked my quotations. He'd never had a college boy fight as a pro, and now he was having a new experience. He also praised my strength to various and sundry people, and I don't think it was before my fifth or sixth bout as a light heavyweight that I realized that this wasn't exactly what you'd call 100 percent praise. It was a little bit like praising a lawyer for having a loud voice, or complimenting a civil engineer for never forgetting to wear a necktie when he had to give a report before the city council.

Not that a boxer doesn't have to be strong, and not that sheer physical bodily strength isn't an asset . . . but the fact is, prizefighters are not weight lifters, and beyond a certain point, sheer bodily strength (the kind required to lift your opponent around and shove him into the ropes) will only take you so far in this business; and in itself, it won't even get you near a top-ten ranking.

In fact, Bertie brought this up one day: he made an effort to clarify all that praise, letting me know that beyond a point strength was as irrelevant as brains.

"Speaking of which," he said, "you gotta stick your man with a jab and do it natural; what you don't wanna do is call a committee together so you can deliberate the issue." (Here, you could tell, Bertie figured he was speaking my language.)

"I'll think about it," I said, nodding. But Bertie didn't pick up on it; my voice was too pure.

My twelfth fight as a light heavy was the last one. I was matched against a tall, caramel-colored man named Luther Otts, who was very fast and very heavy with his fists. The only thing was, he could be tagged—especially by a shorter, inside fighter (me)—and he could be knocked out. In fact, he'd been knocked out eleven times. On the other hand, he'd knocked out about three times that many. He was known as a smoker with a glass jaw—it was either feast or famine with old Luther. I mentioned this fact to Bertie, who said, "Don't give me no proverbs, because I don't care to hear such talk from my athletes."

This was too bad, in view of the fact I was infatuated with information and succinct language, which puts huge ideas into small capsules. But Bertie was uneasy when I resorted to data and epigrams. He figured I was reaching over his head, which was true in a way.

But to get back to Luther Otts, I liked this idea of the number twelve. It seemed significant to me; I was going for my twelfth fight as a light heavy, and Luther was going for his twelfth time to be knocked out. We were both coming together at some mystical number—twelve.

I would have explained this to Bertie, but he wouldn't have listened. If Bertie hadn't invented tunnel vision, he'd come close to perfecting it. He had never even asked what I was studying in college. He probably thought everybody took the same courses, the way he'd done it in elementary school.

And yet Bertie had a goofy dignity and, in its way, a mind. He might have been one of the few people who really think about things, in a tunnel or out.

But I should get back to Luther Otts, which you can see I'm having trouble doing because it's not a pleasant thing to do. Not even in memory. The fact is, Luther knocked me out in the sixth round, halfway to twelve, even though it was only a ten-round fight. He gave me the kind of beating that could turn a man to religion. He beat me to the punch so often, I might as well have had cement blocks wired to my fists.

And it all happened because Luther had perfected a right cross that caught me every time I tried to jab him. Bertie hadn't told me about this cross. Ray Evers didn't tell me about it. Neither did Otis Treib or Phil LaCosta. Nobody told me about it, and by the time I might have figured it out, I was so blurred from Luther's head shots I couldn't have identified my own driver's license.

Finally, I regained consciousness with my mouthpiece half out of my mouth on the canvas and the toes of the referee about eighteen inches before my eyes. I figured Luther was probably eating dinner somewhere, trying to remember what I'd looked like before the fight. I pictured him drinking water from a glass, then shaking his head and saying, "Why does that damn Bertie *do* things like that?"

Referring to what he had to consider an awful mismatch, of course.

This was my last prizefight, but I didn't realize it right away, even though I'd been so badly beaten. It isn't often you can immediately recognize the last time you've done something. Think about it.

But after the Otts fight, there was a problem: for the next two weeks, I could hear whispering inside my head every now and then, when the world got quiet. But I could never figure out what the whispering said.

Was I scared? You bet I was. I was terrified of that voice that would whisper things to me when nobody was around to hear. I knew it was only in my head, but in my head was enough. It was like there was somebody inside my brain who wanted me to know something, but he couldn't talk out loud; so I couldn't figure out what it was he was trying to say.

But in spite of this, that fight with Luther Otts left me with the conviction that I could beat him if I ever got into the ring with him again, because that unorthodox hook of his could be blocked with no problem, if you were expecting it . . . the problem was, as I've said, I wasn't expecting it until Luther had pounded my head so numb I couldn't have sharpened a pencil or opened my wallet. I knew I was stronger than Luther, and I could probably punch him out within three or four rounds if I could find his button without having my own head hammered and tenderized.

When the doctor gave me the okay and I came back to the gym to work out again, I talked with Bertie about this. I analyzed the whole business for him: one, two, three.

He listened and chewed his gum and stared thoughtfully at a new welterweight that he'd put over on the speed bag. Once, when I figured his attention had drifted a little too much, I actually got up the nerve to poke him on the shoulder with my index finger, so he'd look back at me and take in what I was saying. This was a considerable shock, because *nobody* touched Bertie; standing still, he had too much footwork. But now he seemed to survive the experience.

Finally, I told him about Gene Tunney, Archie Moore, and Mickey Walker. Sure, I was a college boy, I said, but I could take it and dish it out with the rest of them. Didn't Bertie himself say I was as strong as a horse?

Bertie seemed to come partly awake at the familiar words, and he stopped chewing his gum. He narrowed his eyes and, after glancing once again at the new welterweight, he looked back at me and patted my shoulder. Then, in a hoarse whisper, he said, "Forget it."

"Forget it?"

Bertie winked and nodded. "That's the message, kid. You had your fling, now go home and enjoy it. Or back to the classroom, whatever."

I wasn't sure what that meant, but I did it anyway. That is, I went back to my apartment and thought about it.

It was a mystery, and it didn't help any when the whispering came back that night, shortly before I dropped off to sleep. I couldn't make out what it was trying to say, but I had to admit that finally I could recognize the voice: it was Bertie's. The fact was, I'd never heard him whisper before that afternoon, and people don't really sound the same when they whisper.

You'd think they do, but they don't.

These were bad times for me, although I had money. This was one of the reasons I gave for fighting professionally; to get money in a way that was unthinkable to my family. They weren't athletes of any sort. In my freshman year at the university, physical education was required, so I signed up for boxing, because I thought it might be interesting to hit somebody. To my surprise, I could hit harder and faster than anyone else. I was invincible; I broke ribs and noses, even with sixteen-ounce gloves—even when the coach told me to pull my punches. There was something wrong with me. It was too easy.

I had had a falling-out with my family over a matter I won't go into, so here was an opportunity for me to *be on my own*. When they heard I was going to fight as a middle-weight, they were shocked. I heard all about it from my Aunt Teresa, who was only seven years older than I and had never gotten along with my mother, her oldest sister.

Now (jump ahead two years) I was no longer employed. I had $700 in the bank (Bertie had thrown me in over my head—it could have been argued—long before Luther, but I had lucked out), a broken love affair with a college girl named Connie Rinshapen (her wealthy father was Dutch and owned an orchard in Connecticut), and a determination to keep making it on my own. Where was I headed? Somewhere in the future, with luck—beyond that, I didn't much care.

There are waves in a prizefight: by tacit consent, two boxers will fall into a rhythm of rising and falling, of violent exertion and recovery. That is, if they are evenly matched. It's a little like conversation or dancing or even the stride people tend to fall into when they are walking together.

This is more mysterious than it seems on the surface; it extends to the duration level of your life, and you ride the ground swells and breakers along with the inscrutable arrangement of events that pulse through everybody's time. So when things seem to round out and slow down, and you feel that momentary silence like a period or perhaps the eye of a hurricane, wait for the advent. You won't generate it; it will be coasting toward you with its own silent speed, as swift as a breaker gathering out beyond the surf.

For me, it came with a phone call one night when I was sitting in front of the television set, watching a rerun of "Hogan's Heroes."

The phone rang four times before I answered. I remember this: from prizefighting I had learned to count things. The count was always important.

When I answered, I heard Connie Rinshapen's voice. It had been over a year, and I was surprised. In fact, she sounded a little surprised, herself, even though she had been the one to phone.

She asked all the obvious things: how was school, how was my love life, how was my prizefighting career. This last was some sort of climax, because it had been an issue in our breaking up. Connie had believed that I was just trying to be *macho* (a hopeless malaprop, she pronounced it *mock-o*, as if she'd never once heard the word, only seen it in places like the *New Republic* or the *Yale Review*).

I told her I wasn't sure about my career in the ring, and in the silence which followed, I heard a little flurry of whispering in my head. (Maybe it *wasn't* Bertie's whisper; it was hard to tell.) Connie said she was sure I would come to my senses. This was in her earnest voice, which she only used when she was frowning. She was a little bit daffy, but intriguing. I'd always thought so.

"And how's *your* life been?" I finally asked.

She plopped a little gasp of a sigh into the telephone, and I knew this had to do with her call—whatever it was.

"I've been married," she said slowly, "and divorced. Somebody you don't know, by the name of Ron."

"Ron," I said in the manner of one who is tasting the familiarity of a name (like "Stanley Ketchel" or "Tommy Burns").

But Connie missed the implication. "You don't know him from atom," she said.

"Well, whoever he is, that's pretty quick work."

"What is?"

"Getting married and divorced within a year."

I could almost hear her nod. "It was more like an annulment. In fact, that's what it was."

"Or maybe no fault," I suggested, knowing how treacherous language was to Connie.

"That's really the nutshell situation," she said, missing the legal nuance.

"Well, it's still fast work. You didn't even know this Ron when we were going together, did you?"

"No, I didn't know him from atom. But I was infatuated. He came into my life like a hurricane. You know."

"Sure."

"He infatuated me," she repeated, liking the success of it.

"That happens sometimes."

"Listen," she said, "could we see each other, do you think? I've got an absolutely humongous sort of favor to ask."

"Sure."

"How about lunch tomorrow? On campus. Would that be okay? You know, the usual place?"

"Sure."

"And something else," she said, before hanging up. "I'm glad you're cooling off about prizefighting. And please don't try to defend it to me: I can remember your arguments like they were yesterday. But I'm just not convinced. I'm just one of those people who don't happen to look upon prizefighting as either an art or a science, so don't bother wasting your breath on that old issue again."

"I won't," I said.

"Listen, you're too fine a person to end up being just another punch drunkard."

"Right," I said, impressed by Connie's insight, as well as her way of expressing herself. As always.

The place where we ate was a campus cellar joint named Trucker Ed's, and even though it was hardly bigger than a three-car garage, there were usually about fifty or sixty customers at lunchtime.

Connie looked just fine, it seemed to me. She is a slender, airy, beautiful blonde with long, wispy hair—the sort who makes deodorant commercials (running slow-motion through a field, maybe), because she doesn't look as if she could smell bad even if she tried. It was a cold day, and Connie had a thick tan scarf thrown around her neck, letting her hair fly loose.

We settled down at a booth next to the window, and knowing how hard it was to get a window booth, Connie said, "Well, it looks like we're two of the elected today."

I agreed that it might be a good sign of something and ordered two beers and pastramis on rye. She didn't contradict me. Some things abide.

We chatted on a variety of topics, but all the time I could sense

35

Connie's approach to the Subject, whatever it was. I knew the way she worked, and was intrigued. Whenever she mentioned something or somebody, I made a mental check, eliminating it from consideration as having any relevance to this favor she was about to ask. She was daffy, but not simple.

With the last bite of her pastrami, her eyes changed. Slowly she chewed and gazed out the window upon the campus. Then she swallowed. This was it.

"It's about Ron," she said.

"Your ex-husband, right?"

"Right. He's a problem."

"In what way?"

She cast her look upward and thought. "He's got these things that belong to me, and he won't let me have them back. I mean, they're *mine*. They always have been. And how he can think he has a right to just sit on them and *possess* them individually, like his very own, joggles the imagination."

"You mean, boggles."

"All right: *boggles,* if it makes you happy. I don't know what it means, anyway, so what difference does it make?"

I thought about that a moment and then said, "What sort of things?"

Connie inhaled with her eyes raised—a sign of exasperation. "Oh, some necklaces and rings and things. You know, jewels."

"Are they valuable?"

"I suppose so. Sure, some of them. But it's their sentimental value that's important." She thought a moment and added: "Well, *both.*"

"I'd think they would have been the first things you took with you when you left," I said. "People grab their jewels even if they bail out of a hotel window when there's a fire."

Connie shook her head. "You'd think so, wouldn't you? But some people do dumb things sometimes, under stress, and I'm one of those people, I guess. It was so ugly when we broke up, I just left. If I'd been naked, I wouldn't have thought to get dressed. It's a wonder I remembered my purse, even. I was in an emotional storm, thoroughly destroyed."

I sipped at my beer and thought about ordering another one. Connie's mug was almost empty too, but with more beer she might be even harder to pin down.

"That's where you come in," she said.

"Where?"

"According to the law, I'm entitled to retrievership. I've discussed this with an attorney friend, and he agrees in principle, 100 percent."

Some lawyer, if he knew Connie, I thought. But I kept quiet.

"Don't you want to know where you come in?" she asked, reaching over and clasping my wrist. I loved her chin and jaw line, which are an important part of a woman's beauty.

"I'm almost afraid to ask," I said.

She nodded. "I want you to come with me. That's all. Just come along, and then if Ron tries anything, you can put a halt to it right then and there."

"You mean belt him one?"

Connie considered that. "No, I don't think it has to come to that sort of crisis, if you know what I mean. I think that just with you being there and sort of looking after me, Ron will take the hint and not try anything funny."

The decision wasn't very difficult; Connie had her problems, all right, but dishonesty wasn't one of them. "Sure, I'll give you a hand," I said.

"Oh, thanks!" she said, grabbing my wrist again. "I knew I could depend on you. Is this evening all right?"

"Sure. Strike while the iron is hot."

"Exactly!"

"I only hope he doesn't cause trouble," I said.

For some reason, the idea bothered me. The thought of uncontrolled violence was disturbing. I liked mine by the rules. Or at least, *had*.

I tried to explain this to Connie, and she listened politely, but I could tell her thoughts were elsewhere. Probably with Ron and her jewels.

Later on, she said something that surprised me a little. I'd finally ordered another beer for us, and halfway through the mug, Connie said, "Actually, he kind of frightens me."

"Ron does?"

She nodded. "He's sort of irrational, if you know what I mean. That was the major trouble between us. Not the only one, but the greatest major one."

"That should be enough," I said.

My thought was that we should go over to Ron's apartment (which had once been hers as well) when he was there. Just go up and knock on the door and walk in and get Connie's jewels. But Connie preferred subtler tactics. She said that Ron always ate dinner out and never got home until nine or ten at night. Or practically never. Only sometimes he came back in the afternoon to get something or take a shower. So the safest time would be around six o'clock.

"Do you still have a key?"

"I certainly do," Connie said. "Only I need reinforcements to go back in there. You don't know what Ron is like. He's practically a soddist."

I ordered another beer. It was good being back with Connie. I had missed her. And when I told her that I'd decided to give up prize-fighting, she said that was very prudent of me. Not only that, she said it right.

As for me, after a few beers, I could feel that whispering start to tune up in my head. I decided to give up on the beer, and Connie agreed, so we went to a nearby restaurant and had spaghetti, which sobered me up all right and put Connie in a quiet and mysterious mood.

But soon it was time to go to Ron's place, so we got a cab and Connie sat on the edge of the seat, making random observations about politics and telling the driver where to turn. The driver was a small, bushy-haired man with thick glasses and a pencil behind his ear. When I glimpsed his face in the rearview mirror, I saw that his lips were moving silently. Connie could do that to people; I've seen it happen many times.

The apartment verged on the classy; it was pale brick with heavy, blood-red shutters and flowering trees planted in raised drums throughout the courtyard. Now the trees were all barren, but the effect remained. Ron must be doing all right, although this could be Connie's money still at work, I pictured him as the type who'd take alimony from a woman.

When we went in the appropriate doorway, Connie started breathing hard, and I knew she was nervous. I managed to stay pretty calm, since I looked upon this as her business, not mine; I was only along to keep the peace, in a manner of speaking. Although this might include popping Ron, if he was as irrational as Connie said. I didn't like that part. And maybe he had a gun; even worse.

I was about to ask Connie if she wanted me to open the door. She was fumbling at a battery of locks as big as a slot machine. But right then the door swung open, and Connie darted in before I had a chance to look up and down the hallway. It was a nice interior. I told her so. Then I mentioned that I had always liked nice things; I wasn't sure I had conveyed this truth to her back in the old days.

Connie remained silent, and after I had chatted a bit, I realized that I was still feeling the beer and would be better off silent. A slight sound at the front of the apartment caused me to turn around just in time to see the front door swing open, showing a large, beefy fellow standing there with a leather jacket over his arm and his tie loosened about his neck. He looked as if he had been preparing for a quick nap while he'd been walking down the hall.

His mouth opened and he was obviously about to say, "What in hell is this!" when I heard Connie behind me say, "Oh, God, Ron!" She ran the words together, giving an interesting ambiguity to the exclamation.

"Just don't move a step!" Ron said.

I turned and saw that Connie was holding a small jewelry box close to her bosom. She was also panting, wild-eyed. "It's mine!" she whispered. "And you know it!"

"That remains to be seen," Ron said warily, closing the door softly behind him.

I half expected Connie to say, "Pop him now!" But she didn't, for which fact I was grateful. I didn't like the idea a bit. Bertie Gunnerman would have understood.

After a moment's study, Ron said to her, "I take it that this is your ex-boyfriend. The boxer?"

Connie nodded.

"Well, kindly inform him on my behalf," Ron said, "that his fists are considered lethal weapons."

"I ain't gonna pop nobody," I said, resorting to stereotyped dialogue.

Ron nodded gravely, then turned back to Connie. "So you think you have a right to break and enter, just so you can retrieve your costume jewelry. I should have had the locks changed."

"It's not costume jewelry, and you know it." Connie said.

Refusing to answer, Ron merely closed his eyes. But when he opened them, he surprised both of us. "Take it and get out," he muttered. "Now. Before I change my mind."

"It's not yours to change," Connie said, which like many of her utterances was as interesting as it was off target.

"What she means," I said, "is that the jewelry isn't yours to dispense with."

Ron closed his eyes again. "I know what she means," he said. "Don't you think I had to learn the goddamn language in all those months I was married to her?"

I was about to respond to this, when Connie grabbed my arm and hurried me out of the apartment.

We went to the local McDonald's, where Connie said she wanted to get two things: her breath and a cup of coffee.

We went inside, and while she took a seat next to the window, I got the cups of coffee from the counter and took them over to her.

She was smiling. "I can't believe it was that easy," she said, caressing the cup.

I nodded and sat down. I started to take a sip, and then I heard some fast whispering. For a couple of minutes I sort of blacked out, and when I came to, Connie was saying, "I think you intimated Ron. I honestly do!"

Then we were both surprised (me, mostly) when I reached over and popped Connie on her neat little chin with my fist, and she dropped like a bag of nickels in her seat.

As long as I live, I'll never forgive myself for what I did that day. Also, I'll never understand why I did it. I think Luther Otts shook something loose in my head, because I have always believed that there is nothing more contemptible than a man hitting a woman. I don't care what she does or what she says (which is usually worse than anything she can *do*, but never mind that).

Some people would say that what I did was forgivable. They'd point out that Connie was just put out like a light (as they used to say), and came around with no more buzz in her head than if she'd taken a little nap. She told me so. There was only a little sore bruise on her chin, which (as I mentioned) I considered lovely beyond words. That, and her cheek.

But I can't let it go at that. What it was, I pushed a button, and the ringing still lasts. Not whispering in my ears but ringing. I speak of reality and marriage. Because, what could be more of a cliché than what happened to us: Connie sort of looking at me with different eyes, after that, and my wanting to make it up to her forever.

It's true, all of it. Reality lies inside the clichés, not beyond them. Ask anybody who has thought about it. (I almost said, ask Bertie Gunnerman; but that would be getting ahead of what I have to tell.)

Ugly. Stupid. Taboo. All three, and then some. Why else would I have to tell about it? (Talk about buttons!) And of all the things in this world I could have chosen to do, popping Connie like that would have been the last, *could I have chosen.*

The shock must have been considerable. For a while, she even talked right; she didn't sound like Connie. (I would have guessed she'd repeat what Jack Sharkey said after he'd been knocked out by Jack

Dempsey: "It felt like I'd fallen into a transom.") But the shock was psychological; Connie told me so and forgave me. She could see how miserable I was over the whole business. I even felt bad about the hot coffee that had splashed over her lap, giving slight burns to her tender parts, not to mention upper thighs.

God, the shame of it! And here I was so uptight about the risk of popping Ron! Maybe that was part of it, I argued in my head. (The whispering gradually disappeared, and I hardly ever blacked out after that.) What I meant was, I was so intent upon holding back in one context that I had to pay for it in another. "Drive out nature with a pitchfork," as Ruby Bob Fitzimmons used to say, quoting Terence, "and she'll return on both sides."

The world is full of scapegoats and taboos. Look around, and you'll see them everywhere. Look inside. "Fool, look into thy heart and write." (I don't know who said that, but it sounds enough like a cliché to have some truth in it.)

Chekhov said: "Everybody has something to hide." This was in one of his notebooks. And it is true. Ron has something to hide; so does Connie (but I doubt if she knows it). Bertie Gunnerman has much to hide: how could it be otherwise, when he has given so much advice to so many people? And how about Luther Otts? Much to hide.

Which brings me to one of the constants in this account: I still believe I could beat him. Or could have, back when we were young enough to engage in such folly. I followed his career for a while, and he didn't amount to much. I could have gone farther— maybe about fifty yards, but no more. I didn't have the instincts or the quickness, which are two indispensables for Bertie's sport.

Speaking of which and whom, I came across him one day in a men's clothing store. He was trying on a Harris Tweed jacket, and I went up to him and poked the back of his shoulder. "Bertie," I said.

He was facing into a triptych mirror, and I saw his eyes readjust in the center one, so that he could see me. I must have looked the same reversed, because he said, "Well, hello, Athlete."

"College Boy," I prompted him.

Bertie turned around. "That's right," he said, poking me back with his finger, right in front of where I'd poked him. "Middleweight and then light heavy," he said, reminiscing. "Two-one-one as the former, and eight-three-one as the latter."

"Fantastic remembering, Bertie," I told him. I knew that would make him proud, even though it was true.

"I remember my athletes," he said, shaking his head.

Very impressive, I thought, but does he *really* remember me, or just my record?

As if hearing my thought, Bertie got a distant, thoughtful look on his face. "I well remember," he said reminiscently; "I can see you now, out there in the middle of the ring, *meditating*."

"Lou Nova, too," I said.

This was the old Bertie, all right. He thought a moment and nodded. "One of the worst sinners of all," he said. "Not to mention, slow of hand and without conviction. A Hollywood type, which he became."

"I'm looking for a sweater," I said. "I need a new sweater. I was figuring on a shawl neck."

For a moment we were silent. Then Bertie said, "You know something, pal? I should have kept you as a middleweight. You'd've done fine as a middle. With maybe some changes in attitude. I liked your strength, but you didn't take head shots so good."

"Too late now, Bertie," I said.

"Too late for a lot of things," Bertie said, shrugging the Harris Tweed jacket to see how it fit in the shoulders.

So that's the way I left him, looking at himself in the triptych mirror. I was on my way home, where Connie was waiting.

All the way on the bus, I kept thinking about how I should tell my story. Finally I decided: one, two, three. How else? Remember the count. This is something I learned in the ring (and don't think I'm talking about your being knocked down and having the referee count over you; I'm somewhere else in this thing).

There's only one detail I need to clear up. A mistaken impression, no doubt. Somewhere earlier in my story, I said I'd become a professional boxer because of money. But that's not precisely the case.

The fact is, I don't know why I became a boxer. It had something to do with *machismo*, sure, but there was so much more to it than that, I couldn't explain it if I devoted a whole book to the issue.

What it was, was a sort of blackout, like when I popped Connie. At one time I'd concluded that the ugly episode in McDonald's that day was the only truly spontaneous thing I'd ever done. But then, when I would think of whatever had prompted me to become a professional boxer, I would come upon a blankness as deep as that little nap I'd taken when my fist had gone out and popped her on the chin. Darkness all around. Underneath, too; only the shaft of light from above (the present time) where we are trying to see it clearly.

Some people don't have a gift for the spontaneous, and it looks like I'm one of them. But it's more than this: I figure that there are

42

mysterious bureaucracies in the mind that make our great decisions, and we don't preside over them any more than a drunken committee chairman presides over a congregation of puppies.

Connie had her own version of this insight, which I'd purchased with considerable confusion and shame. I kept fantasizing a scene when the two of us would be sitting over a glass of wine, perhaps— feeling meditative and talking about the old days. The issue of my failure as a pugilist would come up, along with the related issue of my general incapacity for the spontaneous. I can almost see her lift the wine glass, caress its stem, and say in a broody voice: "It just isn't your meteor."

"Which is true," I would say, "our faults being not in our stars but in ourselves."

Connie would ride that out all right, and then we would go on to other things, whatever they might be.

THE BRANCH OFFICE
IN PRAGUE

Hotel Maria Theresa
38 Novotny Square
Praha
Nov. 6, 1911

Herr Karl Pilscher, President
Fels and Nurtzwanger Co.
111 B Willemstrasse EB
Berlin

Dear Esteemed President, Herr Pilscher:

I am writing to you after receiving my latest report from Johann
Spatny, whom you will remember as our Branch Manager in Prague.
I have received this report in person, although it does not strike me
as being fully satisfactory. No doubt, you will recall the situation
clearly: one of Mr. Spatny's salesman, Mr. Gregor Samsa, has missed
a number of appointments and does not seem to be available for ques-
tioning at this time. You know, of course, about Mr. Samsa's recent
sales performance, but I will recapitulate: he has been with us four
years, with an exemplary record until some six months ago, when his
sales began to show a sharp decline. Mr. Spatny has taken a special
interest in his case, but [I can't help adding at this time] an even
greater interest in Mr. Samsa's very attractive young sister.

But to the issue at hand: Spatny has informed me, Esteemed President, that Gregor Samsa has suffered a mental breakdown of the most serious nature. If we were back in Vienna, I would be inclined to suggest that he consult with Dr. Freud there, whose neurological investigations have excited world-wide interest. But this is of course impossible, and we must do what we can with whatever [and whoever] is available. So I have suggested Dr. Kohar, a local neurologist of proven reputation.

Spatny has not responded to my suggestion. He admits to knowing of Dr. Kohar's reputation in the treatment of neurological and "mental" problems, but seems to think that young Samsa will not respond to any treatment Dr. Kohar can provide. Why? Well, you must believe me when I say, My Dear Sir, that I am not jesting with you when I state that, according to Spatny, Gregor Samsa has become convinced that he is some kind of insect, a gigantic Cockroach, in fact. Can you believe it? I wonder if Dr. Freud himself has ever heard of anything so extravagant! Still, our Spatny will not budge: that is his story. Meanwhile, he has been seen with Samsa's sister, Grete, at the opera. They say the two of them were there only last night, during a performance of *Le Nozze de Figaro*. How must the poor girl have felt attending an opera with her brother's Branch Manager [to whom her family owes considerable money] while that brother was himself lying at home paralyzed with the notion that he had been transformed into some sort of giant vermin [evidently, he is inconsistent as to the precise entomological details] and utterly incapable, at this time, of resuming his responsibilities with our company, and thereby earn a livelihood for this very sister, not to mention their father and mother?

I am writing at such great length to you, Herr Pilscher, because, as you will remember, we have discussed young Samsa's career before. In fact, you asked about him at our last meeting, so I know you are eager to hear whatever I can learn about him.

Also, there's Spatny. I am quite worried about him. He has proved an excellent Branch Manager, and yet . . . well, I can hardly put it into words, but my last interview with him was very disconcerting. "There is something Spatny is holding back," I told myself. And that is precisely the impression I got. Of course, there's his 'old trouble with young women,' as the joke has it. But in addition, it saddens me to state, Esteemed President, that at ten o'clock in the morning our Faithful Spatny smelled like a distillery. Brandy, if I mistake not, and French brandy, at that.

Well, this is sufficient for now. I have written enough for two letters, so I shall close. But be assured, I will keep in touch re: the Samsa/Spatny affair.

Most Respectfully Yours,
Herr President,

Franz Duba
Regional Manager

Fels & Nurtzwanger Co.
111 B Willemstrasse EB
Berlin
Nov. 18, 1911

Franz Duba, Regional Manager
Fels & Nurtzwanger
c/o Hotel Maria Theresa
38 Novotny Square
Prague

My Dear Duba:

Yours of Nov. 6 received, during my absence for business reasons in Danzig. Our company has attenuated with growth, which [attenuation] we must all resist with all our might.

Of course I remember young Samsa, and remember asking about him. Furthermore, I recall meeting him when I last visited Prague. Incidentally, Duba, you neglected to state precisely what you were doing there; did you go simply to investigate the Samsa situation?

As for Samsa: the following data present themselves to my memory: he was one of our clerks before "going on the road"; before that, he was a lieutenant in the army; and he has a pronounced lisp. I recall this last detail quite vividly, for upon meeting him, I asked myself: "What do Spatny and Duba mean by promoting this young man to a sales position?"

Still, as you point out, his record until last spring was quite respectable, and we *should let sleeping dogs sleep,* as the English proverb states.

It seems to me you're spending too much time worrying about

Spatny. We must either take him as he is, or find a replacement. He's too old a dog to cure of his itch for females, although I confess to being surprised about his morning drunkenness. Maybe the Samsa girl rejected him. Do you suppose? Is she a good enough item to do that to a man, do you think? I don't recall ever seeing her, although I have met this fellow Gregor, as I've mentioned somewhere above.

It seems to me he's the one we have to figure out. Why don't you go to his flat and face him with the facts? I should think this is what a Regional Manager would think of first when he hears something as bizarre as the story that this drunken lecher Spatny has reported. A gigantic insect, indeed! What won't they think of next, just to avoid a little hard work! It wasn't like this when I started out with Fels and Nurtzwanger, you may be certain.

I expect you to keep me in touch, Duba. With your usual efficiency and attention to detail, Etc.

Yours,

Pilscher
President

Hotel Maria Theresa
38 Novotny Square
Praha
Nov. 27, 1911

Herr Karl Pilscher, President
Fels and Nurtzwanger Co.
111 B Willemstrasse EB
Berlin

Dear Esteemed President, Herr Pilscher:

Your most welcome epistle of November 18 received with gratitude and joy. I am honored that you are taking such an interest in the Samsa Case.

As you suggested, I tried earnestly to gain admittance to the Samsa household, but was turned away as if I had been a street peddler. I warned the old man who stood at the door that young

Gregor's position with Fels & Nurtzwanger was at stake, but he was unmoved by my threats. This old fool was dressed in a shabby uniform of some sort, which I couldn't quite identify. Perhaps he plays the tuba in one of the local bands; or perhaps he is a bank guard. At any rate, I infer that he is Gregor's father, because a beautiful young girl was standing there behind him, staring at me out of great dark eyes, and she referred to him as "Papa." Naturally, I assume that this girl is none other than Gregor's sister, first name Grete. But she was as adamant in refusing me entrance as the old drum major was, so I finally left the premises, muttering to myself.

Still, I'll have to admit, Grete Samsa is the sort of girl that could turn a man's head, not to mention his heart. And if you take a fellow like Spatny, our *esteemed* [irony here, Herr President] Branch Manager, the results must necessarily be unpredictable. Or perhaps, one should say, *predictable.*

Speaking of our Branch Manager: he himself has missed work the past few days. It is only fortunate that I myself happen to be in Prague, for if I weren't, this branch would be in a bad state. You see, I have pitched in to help out with Spatny's duties while he is off. What's wrong with him? Well might you ask. Nobody seems to know, and I have sent errand boys to his apartment every hour, but they all return with the same old answer: no Spatny. I myself went there, of course; but the apartment was empty . . . a fact I can swear to, for the Concierge allowed me to enter and examine the premises. Spatny was not there. I looked for him as hard as if he were no larger than the cockroach poor Samsa evidently thinks he's become.

As for Samsa: rest assured, my Esteemed President, I shall return and find out what has happened to him. Maybe he's in a sanitorium somewhere. However, I think not, for if he were, why would that old fool dressed up in his comic opera General's uniform refuse me admittance?

Please do not trouble yourself: the Prague office is humming along like an electric dynamo. Orders are piling up, and the salesmen [except for Samsa] are all smiles and good humor, with their pockets stuffed to bursting with receipts for new shipments!

Most Respectfully Yours,
Esteemed President,

Franz Duba
Regional Manager
[and Branch Manager pro tem]

Fels & Nurtzwanger Co.
111 B Willemstrasse EB
Berlin

Duba:

Yours of Nov. 27 received. I cannot help but wonder what sort of operation you're running down there. Has the whole city gone mad? Has a plague of lunacy descended upon you? The only wholesome information your latest contained was the reference to Grete Samsa. I am an old man. The world is bewildering enough, without your adding to the evidence that it's "bound for hell in a basket," as the English like to say.

You will, of course, be expected to keep me informed. And naturally I don't ask you to conceal the truth from me. I just ask for better news, that's all. Little enough for an old man to ask, one would think. Sometimes I wonder why I ever accepted the Presidency of Fels and Nurtzwanger, knowing what I did of its widespread activities, army of sales people, and proclivity for disaster of the baroque and unexpected kind.

Yours,

Pilscher
President, F & N

Hotel Maria Theresa
38 Novotny Square
Praha
Dec. 12, 1911

Herr Karl Pilscher, President
Fels and Nurtzwanger Co.
111 B Willemstrasse EB
Berlin

Honored President, Herr Pilscher:

Receiving your letter has lightened my spirits, Her Pilscher! I laughed aloud at your wit and whimsy, fully recognizing while doing so the seriousness behind every turn of phrase!

You are, of course, perfectly correct, as usual. Things are appallingly confused here, and it is only by titanic effort that we are able to sustain the interests of Fels & Nurtzwanger in the City of Prague! I thank our stars that I happened to be "on the scene" when all burst loose, for if I had had to travel here from my home office, everything might have gone to pieces by the time of my arrival, no matter how swiftly I flew!

Herr Pilscher, I have spoken with Spatny! He has returned to us, loyally reporting to his office after an ordeal that is . . . well, astonishing. I fear that things are even worse than your jocular references would suggest.

You will no doubt recall that Spatny told me that Herr Samsa was suffering from some kind of terrible mental disorder that had left him with the illusion that he had been transformed into a gigantic cockroach; well, now the truth is out, and it is worse even than we suspected. Because—can you believe it, Herr President?—Spatny himself claims he witnessed Gregor Samsa *in the form of a huge insect,* and that the creature tried to communicate with him, as if it were trying to speak in a human voice! [Here, Spatny began to give some kind of grotesque imitation of the squeaking noise, until I made him desist.]

Spatny wept after he'd revealed this monstrous hallucination, Herr President, and I comforted the poor miserable wretch as best I could, but what, when all is said and done, *could* I do? Fraulein Biltner, his old secretary, signalled one of the boys, who went out to fetch a policeman, and within the hour there was a medical staff there in our headquarters, carrying poor Spatny away in a strait-jacket! Fraulein Biltner wailed in duet with Spatny, and before long the entire office staff was weeping, as well. I have never witnessed such an orgy of grief and terror.

Why was there such panic? Because Spatny had shared his monstrous delusion with everyone who had ears, there were a dozen reports that he'd stopped people upon the street, grabbed their lapels or the collars of their coats, and yelled out at them every detail of his incredible hallucination!

Today, the office is quiet as a tomb. Fraulein Biltner's sniffling has ceased, and an awful quiet prevails where once there were all the manifold sounds of a happy Branch office. I can still hear poor Spatny's screaming, however, and wonder how long it will echo in my memory. No doubt poor loyal Fraulein Biltner feels the same way, for she has a stricken air about her.

You ask: what is happening in this city, and from the deepest portion of my heart, I answer you, Esteemed President: I don't know! Spatny seemed as sane as you or I [well, at least as I] only a month ago: now look what has happened to him!

All this transpired only yesterday, Herr Pilscher [if you will allow me to address you so informally, for I feel the need of your strength in a moment like this, and throw myself upon your mercy].

We look everywhere for signs, but what's to be done? I cannot find it in my heart to return to Gregor Samsa's flat and once again face that mad old man, his Father, dressed in the uniform of a circus attendant. As for his beautiful sister . . . my heart goes out to her, and I only wish that God will somehow provide for her. It is her face that appears to me at odd moments, and I whisper: *Be happy, Angel! Be happy!*

Is it any wonder, Esteemed President, that we are virtually unstrung?

Respectfully Yours,

Franz Duba

Fels & Nurtzwanger Co.
111 B Willemstrasse EB
Berlin

Duba:

Yours of the 12th Dec. arrived, finding me in utter perplexity and leaving me in same. What you referred to by my "wit and whimsy" is beyond my conceiving. I have never joked in letters, and do not intend to start now. Have you taken up Spatny's ways with French Brandy? Or has the Prague plague of madness swept you away, along with everybody else in that benighted place? [Note: these are questions that require no answer, especially not of your long-winded sort.]

I cannot conceive of how anybody could let a branch office disintegrate beneath his very hands the way you have let our Prague office disintegrate. You are the captain of our ship there, Duba, and you had better not forget it. If the Prague branch goes down, you go down with it. If there is an "abandon ship," you had better be the last one off, and the ship had better make it safely into port *anyway,* with or without your guidance. Do I make myself clear? [I should have said "misguidance," but my secretary would have tried to correct me, thinking me more senile than I think I am.]

I want no more bad news from Prague. I cannot tolerate the thought of same. No bad jokes, either, Duba. Learn this lesson well: no jokes from me; no jokes from you. This is the way to get on in the world, not to mention that part of it which concerns the two of us, namely Fels and Nurtzwanger.

What in Heaven's name is an old President to do? Is the world coming apart? They're dancing mad in Danzig, and plagued in Prague. [That is not a joke, Duba; do not treat it as such.] Vienna holds its own, but then they are crazy enough there that they won't know the rest of the world is crazy until it's all over. Too late, if you grasp my meaning.

Yours,

Pilscher
President, F & N

Hotel Maria Theresa
38 Novotny Square
Praha

Herr Karl Pilscher, President
Fels and Nurtzwanger Co.
111 B Willemstrasse EB
Berlin

My Honored President, Herr Pilscher:

Never, upon my most sacred word of honour, could I find it in my soul to mock the least of your words, or to interpret your letters humorously. When I last wrote to you, dictating the letter to Fraulein

Biltner [who may have misinterpreted a word or two, she is so understandably upset], I was suffering from a truly physical *disability*, the beginnings of an *influenza*, which I now, thank Heaven, have survived. The disease rages throughout the city, and no one seems to be able to withstand it. Christmas, that time of joy, will be a grim one for many in this awful, cold place with its great wide streets buffeting with gusts of wind, and its gray buildings standing like prisons as far as the eye can see.

Terrible dreams visited me in my sickness, Herr Pilscher, but I will not complain to you, even though you have always been as a [somewhat distant] father to me, if the truth be known. But never mind that. You ask for good news, and I shall give you some.

Do you remember Gregor Samsa? I don't have copies of my letters to you with me at the moment, but it seems to me I have written to you about him. Spatny, of course. I'm certain I've kept you in touch with his tragic fate. [They say he's still raving, sealed up like a jar of sauce in the hospital at St. Ravenna.]

Anyway, I saw his sister, Grete, today. [I mean Samsa's.] And do you know something? She was more beautiful than ever. I asked about her, and Fraulein Biltner [whom I'd asked, naturally] told me that she'd heard that the exquisite creature was now working in a shop in this very neighborhood! Can you believe it?

Herr President, I am not well. I am the first to admit this. Something is going around. I have the feeling that there are beaded curtains before my eyes, but I can't quite brush them out of the way. The fate of poor Spatny preys upon my mind. That crazy old general in his dirty and mussed uniform . . . what is such a creature as that *doing* in this world? And what about Spatny? I keep asking myself. What about Spatny?

But let us think of something pleasant. Grete Samsa passed by our office this evening, on her way home. It was almost dark, and some of the flats nearby have Christmas candles already lighted in them. I went up to her and spoke. Do you know what I said? I wish I could tell you. But that, after all, is not important, Herr Pilscher: what is important is this: she gazed upon me with the most peaceful expression I have ever seen, and finally she actually smiled at me! I am in love, Pilscher! In love! I begged her with tears in my eyes to come to my room, and she accepted.

Herr President, it would be ungracious of me to tell you what we did, so I won't say a word. She lifted the back of her hair like a gift and then let it down, driving me crazy with its heavy loose darkness. She turned to me and kissed the air, speaking some word

I could not hear in my excitement. She removed her clothing and the whiteness of her body blinded me. And the smells . . . oh, Pilscher, the smells! A rich dark garden of love, and do you know something? She has little curls of dark hair in front of her ears, and they are moist. Moist, do you hear? Moist. Spatny had seen all this, you see. We owe much in this world to poor Spatny.

She plays the violin exquisitely, and is cultured in a way you would hardly believe. And when we were in bed, she spoke to me in three languages: German, French, and Slovak. Maybe four. There might have been a fourth language, although I couldn't figure it out, because I was too maddened with lust, Pilscher you old Idiot! Lust! Guilt! Grete Samsa, who whispered to me when we were finished, that her brother had lost all his hair.

Do you know something else she whispered? She said, "Now that is that, and we can go about other things."

"What other things?" I asked her.

And then she said the oddest thing. She said, "Now, we can go somewhere all alone back inside ourselves and spin our webs."

What a curious thing to say, I said to myself, and still say so, again and again. Oh, she is deep, deep, deep!

Oh, yes. I've just this instant received news. Spatny is dead. Hanged himself this morning. Right there in the sanitarium. But our office is all in order, believe me. I could dance a jig, the way I feel now. Grete says her brother has gone away forever. So has Spatny! So shall we all, after the last letter is written and mailed. *Have pity on me, Sir!*

> Respectfully Yours,
> Herr President
>
> Franz Duba

EURO-WIRE

TO: Franz Duba
c/o Hotel Maria Theresa
38 Novotny Square
Prague

FROM: Herr Karl Pilscher
President,
Fels & Nurtzwanger Co.
Berlin

YOUR SERVICES WITH FELS AND NURTZWANGER ARE HEREBY TERMINATED
STOP YOU WILL RECEIVE ALL OVERRIDE AND COMMISSIONS DUE YOU UPON
YOUR APPEARANCE AT HOME OFFICE STOP PRAGUE BRANCH OF FELS AND
NURTZWANGER WILL BE CLOSED EFFECTIVE IMMEDIATELY STOP SEPARATE
WIRE WILL INFORM THOSE IN CHARGE STOP AM NOT YOUR FATHER NEVER
HAVE BEEN NEVER WILL BE STOP

YOURS

KARL PILSCHER, PRESIDENT
FELS AND NURTZWANGER
BERLIN

LOOKING NICE

Scarcely a day passed without Carla Vanderwater's regretting her membership in OASIS, a club for divorced persons. Even the acronym, "Once-Again Singles in Sympathy," bothered her. She thought it both silly and self-consciously clever. The silliness was obvious, but the cleverness was somehow less clear; at moments it seemed there might be something almost sinister in it. She didn't quite know why it bothered her this way, any more than why she thought about it so much. Or, indeed, why she had joined OASIS in the first place.

They met every Wednesday evening (a nothing day, just right for a group like this) in the basement of the St. James Episcopal Church. Eleven women and four men—five, if you included Brad Lassiter, who was a mumbling drunk and seldom came to meetings. The second most miserable night Carla could remember was the night when none of the men showed up, and only six of the women. It wasn't even raining out; just a cold, damp evening. All three of the group's talkers were there, and of course they dominated every second, including the coffee break with instant Folger's and day-old chocolate-chip cookies.

Instead of discussing "those opportunities in life that belonged to them uniquely as single persons" (as the charter instructed), Patti Becker monopolized the conversation with a running commentary on how impossible men were and how little social sense they possessed, as witness their total absence as a gender this evening. Patti was short, broad-shouldered, with terrible dyed-blonde hair (dried clots of bleached seaweed, Candi Thatcher had called it one time). Patti managed the local Burger King, one of the first female managers in the entire system.

A hateful group of misfits. No matter how hard she tried to be charitable, Carla returned again and again to the deadly, dull reality of this fact. One of the women (almost as silent and inscrutable as Carla herself) weighed 320 pounds. This was just about the only fact she shared with the others in a group where sharing was what it was all about. Was her corpulence a symbol of rejection, or had she been fat before her divorce? Another woman—bent, sunken-chested, and lugubriously feminine—had been named "Ned" by her father, who had always wanted a son. Carla knew that many women with men's names accept the fact cheerfully and have no problems with their femininity; but Ned was the predictable exception and used too much eyeshadow and smiled sadly at nothing while others talked.

The men were similarly grotesque in Carla's eyes. There was a fifty-year-old realtor, Hal Hurst, who wore teeny-bopper jeans and had a dyed Prince Valiant haircut. It was really Hal's hair, too, because one evening he'd insisted that everyone give it a tug. Carla and Ned both tried to get out of it, but they finally had to humor him or create a scene, so they both gave Hal's forelock a tentative little pull, relieved that the realtor hadn't insisted they try again and pull harder, as he'd done with Candi Thatcher.

Gary Rickover wasn't bad looking, but he never listened to anybody, and practically all he ever said was: "How about that?" He was smart, in a way, but he had a head like a wind tunnel. He was a computer programmer with a local firm and had the thickest eyebrows Carla had ever seen. Could this be a sign of virility? Was it possible *they* weren't real? Could it be that a man could buy thick eyebrows, like a toupee? Carla asked herself these ridiculous questions several times but decided nothing. Actually, Gary's chin was weak and puckered, and he had soft-looking hands.

Then there were the three talkers—all women and all bright-eyed and hysterical. After her fourth meeting, still feeling like an outsider, Carla was surprised that the men kept coming. If *she* felt out of place, surely *they* must. Then it occurred to her that they might get some sort of perverse pleasure out of hearing women chatter, just to replace the missing noise in their lives. The more she thought about it, the more likely it seemed: these men had all been married to talkers, and came more-or-less faithfully to the OASIS meetings on Wednesday nights so they could store up on female loquacity. And even here (a dark undervoice said in her head) Carla gave no comfort. She was a failure as a woman, even in her inability to keep up a running conversation and afford goofy comfort to divorced men who happened to be neurotic.

In all honesty, Carla felt she was the best of the whole group. She was no beauty, God knew; but she was more nearly normal than anybody else there, and at least she kept her mouth shut without being as pathological about it as, say, Ned or the 320-pound woman, whose name she couldn't remember. (Everybody ignored that poor creature, anyway; she might as well have been a breathing sofa.)

Then there were the talkers. Three out of fifteen (sixteen, if you included Brad Lassiter) would, by statistical probability, do 90 percent of the talking. And two of these three would dominate—the third being a kind of chorus to interpret their confrontations for the benefit of the remainder, the audience.

Carla also believed, quite honestly and without real egotism, that she was the most sensible person there, the most realistic, the most rational. Certainly, she *knew* more than anybody else, if their conversation (or lack thereof) was an indication. Carla read real books— seriously, deeply, thoughtfully (writing down notes in various notepads)—and she doubted if the others read anything more than newspapers or an occasional paperback.

She was of course aware of the darker explanations. Maybe it was precisely their obvious imperfections that kept her coming back: maybe it was just that she'd found a group composed entirely of people she could feel superior to. But this could not be the entire truth, for she was really a nicer person than the sort who'd do something like that. Inferiority, in herself or others, depressed her, and OASIS depressed her more than almost anything she could think of. She would rather watch old movies or reruns on TV, or read the financial news in *U.S. News and World Report,* or talk to a crazy old great-aunt over the telephone, who seemed to hold her responsible for the behavior of her entire generation. Or hear from her ex-husband, Jerry, and savor the historical truth of her having once been married to him, when she'd cooked his breakfast, laughed at his jokes, massaged his back, washed his socks, and ironed his shirts. Not to mention, bear his son . . . only, the boy was more *hers* than his, as anyone could see.

Still, she stuck with it. Carla Vanderwater was not a quitter, even if Patti Becker and Wendy Paulis did go on and on, nonstop, and Gary Rickover chewed his gum and didn't listen, and Candi Thatcher hovered over every word like a kingfisher on a sycamore limb, ready to pounce upon the slightest pause.

Poor Carla just sat and swallowed everything, unable to speak up (which had always been her problem, in marriage and out), letting her face hang out (as Jerry had often criticized her), while people trampled all over her mind, conversationally speaking.

Dumb for all to hear, and without even wiping their dirty feet, she'd added later to herself, embellishing her ex-husband's insult.

The worst evening was the one when Carla actually said something. Somehow, during the interval between Patti's stopping to take a breath and Wendy Paulis's starting in, and before Candi could pounce, Carla gave a little hum, shocking the entire group into silence. It was evident she was going to say something, and even the men took notice.

"I was just going to say," Carla said, as if she had been interrupted, "that I think we all have to live with confusion and inconclusiveness." (Whatever could Patti Becker have said to cue *that* observation?) "Moreover," Carla continued, pausing to clear her throat with a teaspoon-sized cough, "I think we have to learn not only to *tolerate* such things, but learn to *rejoice* in them. I mean, after all, it's confusion and inconclusiveness that we all share, in one form or other. It's our common denominator, don't you see? Isn't it this which has brought us all together? But it has to be more than just us—it's everybody. Therefore, since it's an essential part of the human condition, we should embrace it with all our hearts. *Savor* it! *Rejoice* in it!"

The silence that followed this was a little unnerving, so that later in the evening, Carla was to conclude miserably that it hadn't seemed relevant to anything being discussed at the moment. What else could such a silence mean?

But in a way she realized she shouldn't care. It was something she had believed at the moment; and she had wanted to say it for a long time now. She shouldn't worry about whether Patti, Candi, and Wendy approved or not.

And yet, out of that silence came a signal from an unexpected source. The person who seemed to appreciate her comment the most was none other than Brad Lassiter, who happened to be there that evening—smelling like a brewery, of course, but appearing more or less sober—and kept on nodding long after Carla had finished. She couldn't help wondering how drunk he was. Sometimes when he wasn't too far gone, he gave the impression of being sensitive and maybe even intelligent.

In fact, later that evening he'd actually interrupted Patti Becker, saying, "I think we ought to go back to the point Carla was trying to make."

This seemed to immobilize the entire group, although Candi Thatcher frowned and slapped a wrinkle in her skirt. Carla tried to remember what point she *had* been trying to make, but she was so nervous that she got dizzy; and the next thing she knew, Wendy Paulis had lighted a cigarillo and was pointing it like a dart at poor, silent Ned's sunken chest. "How's come you don't ever say anything?" she said, and Ned's eyes glazed over with embarrassment as she blushed in a dim spasm of miserable self-consciousness.

"I think you're all nuttier than a whole city of fruitcakes," Brad Lassiter said.

Carla couldn't help but appreciate the way he seemed to be taking up for her, and she thought about shooting a brief little smile in his direction, but something stopped her. Maybe fear. Because if there was anything she didn't need in her life at this point in time (as she told herself), it was to get mixed up with a drunk, even if he did have a little style and probably had a lot more to him than, say, Hal Hurst or Gary Rickover.

She tried to think of what Brad did for a living, besides drink, but she couldn't remember. He was actually very well-groomed, when you came to think of it. And then she recalled that somebody—she thought it had been Wendy Paulis, who pretended to know every-thing—had said he owned a chain of laundromats. Or at least, two or three.

There was a lot of money in laundromats, Wendy Paulis had commented.

Carla's ex-husband Jerry was faithful in his alimony payments, but his chronic neglect of their seventeen-year-old boy was indefensible. When she had reproached him for it once, a year ago, Jerry had ex-plained that he was too busy making money so he could keep up his alimony payments to pay attention to his son.

This was typical of him and his quirky logic, so Carla had dropped the subject. As for their son, Tim, he was making her more nervous every day. She worried about him for a variety of reasons, but the sinister thing about it all was that to most people he was just about perfect. Everybody congratulated her on Tim. He was polite, decent, good-looking, earnest, studious, and extremely bright.

Of course these were all virtues in the eyes of any sensible person, including Carla—only somehow they didn't add up to a worry-free life for her. She would watch Tim study or eat his dinner (chewing with his mouth closed) or get ready to go out with some friends (always in by ten o'clock), and she would be afraid. Tim was too good to be true. There was no way she could see for him to go but down. There had to be a catch, somewhere. It wasn't normal for a boy his age to be so mature and decent and well-behaved.

Or, in another mood, she would brood over the fact that she and Jerry didn't deserve such a splendid son. If she was too good for OASIS (which deep in her heart she could not help believing), Tim was too good for her. It was enough to make anyone jumpy, and Carla's nerves had been pretty shaky ever since her divorce.

One of the scariest things about Tim was his success in the stock market, and at the age of seventeen! Jerry had given him a new hundred-dollar bill for Christmas three years ago (the first Christmas after their divorce), suggesting that Tim invest it. *"Invest it!"* Carla had shouted into the telephone while she was reporting upon their conversation to her sister, Rita, and explaining everything: "Here's a fourteen-year-old boy, and Jerry tells him to play the stock market!"

This is exactly what Tim started doing, and at the end of the first year, he had doubled his investment. "Good God," Carla whispered when he made his triumphant announcement. "Do you know that I've read that nine out of ten private investors actually *lose* money when they buy stocks?"

"It's fun," he explained.

"Sure, a barrel of monkeys," she said.

But this was only the beginning. Tim borrowed another hundred from his father, who then repeated the Christmas gift, and within two years, Tim had over a thousand dollars in securities.

From this time on, his investments continued soaring. "Like a rocket," he said, beginning to pick up on the jargon.

The following April there was a feature story about him in the local newspaper, labeling Tim a "Teenage Finance Whiz." Under his photo, he was quoted as saying, "What I've done with pennies, other people can do with dollars."

It was shortly after this that the boy started talking about writing and publishing an investment newsletter.

"They're cropping up all over the place," he told his mother.

"Like mushrooms," she said. "I know all about it. Don't forget, I pick up the mail. You must get a dozen of them yourself."

"I know I'm not rich or anything," Tim said earnestly, frowning at the truth, "but I think my track record is good enough that people just might sit up and take notice."

Carla felt a sudden wave of nausea that reminded her of her only pregnancy, which was now standing in front of her saying these things. No doubt she was too absorbed in her son. She should be a swinger or something. She should leave OASIS and go out and sleep with various men. She should get her mind off Tim, who was secretly driving her crazy.

"Who would you send it to?" she asked, trying to sound interested instead of anxious.

"Friends at school, among others," Tim said, nodding at the good sense of his answer. (*Among others!* Whose child *was* this?)

"I suppose they would tend to trust the advice coming from somebody their own age," Carla said, nodding.

"Exactly," Tim said, catching the beat of her nod and joining her.

"Plus other people, when you get going," Carla said encouragingly.

"You hit the nail on the head," Tim said. "The sky's the limit. A lot of the nickel-and-dime stuff has hit bottom. Which is the time to buy, as everybody knows. And the fact that everybody knows it, means it has to work. You know, a self-fulfilling prophecy."

It was then that Carla realized she had to get a job. Anything to get her out of the house and out of Tim's hair. Or clutches. Whichever. She was a trial to the poor boy, it was obvious. And vice versa. Somehow, her hovering over him was doing deep damage in his psyche, which would all spill out later. Probably in the lap of the poor girl who married him.

Then maybe someday this girl, now divorced, would become a member of the OASIS group and have to listen to Patti and Wendy, grown garrulously old, talk all evening and maybe even have to feel an aged Hal Hurst's hair so that she would know it was real.

The thought threw Carla into a seizure of hysterical humming, which she knew had to seem at least mildly perplexing to her son.

Then, later on, she thought back on the scene and realized he hadn't even seemed to notice; after which she told herself, it really was about time *something* perplexed him, goddamnit!

Brad Lassiter wasn't a drunk after all. He simply drank two bottles of beer before each OASIS meeting, and that was it. He had sleepy pouches around his brown eyes and sort of a big nose that was maybe a little redder than the rest of his face (sunburned from chronic golfing), so it was no wonder that people got the wrong idea. Not only that, he mumbled, probably from latent exasperation at the difficulty of communicating with others.

He wasn't bad looking, once you understood about the drinking, or lack thereof. Carla understood all this one evening when Brad invited her out for a cup of coffee after the session.

"I really like what you said the other night," he told her. "And it wasn't just me. You made them all sit up and take notice. You don't say much, but when you do, it really counts." The two of them were seated by the window in a Wendy's, where Brad was treating her to a single with mustard and ketchup, an order of fries, and a diet Pepsi.

"I haven't eaten all day," she lied, and Brad said, "Well, there's no time like the present." He had ordered a frosty with a cheeseburger on the side.

"I'll tell you something," he told her, "the way Wendy talks, I've almost given up coming to this place—because of the name, you know? *Wendy's.* But what the hell, *she* doesn't own it. Not only that, they've got good cheeseburgers."

Carla almost laughed, assuming that Brad must be joking; but then, seeing the expression on his face, she wasn't sure, so she got her straight face back, chewing seriously.

It did seem an odd place to take a person the first time out, but Brad did things his own way. This evening, he was wearing a zippered-up jogging jacket, blue and white, gray maroon-flecked slacks, and moccasins. Carla wasn't even sure he had a shirt on under the jogging jacket. Evidently, he'd just picked it up and put it on because it was handy. The way he'd chosen Wendy's for their first meal together. Divorced men tended to fall apart like this, she'd heard.

Brad sighed. "I can't take it much longer, you know?"

"Take what much longer?" Carla asked.

"You know what: OASIS. I'm afraid I'm going to have to come up for air." He smiled with one corner of his mouth, but Carla just shook her head.

"You mean quit?" she said.

He nodded and put his straw behind his ear like a pencil. It reminded her of a twelve-year-old boy. She wondered if he'd used the straw, and then remembered that he hadn't. He'd spooned his frosty up. It was too thick for a straw, anyway.

"Me, too," she said distantly.

"You too?"

63

"I'm going to have to find a job," she said darkly. "Or go wacko."

"Wacko? That doesn't sound like a word a girl like you would use."

"Well, it is," Carla said, feeling a little mysterious. "And I'm not exactly what you'd call a girl—I'm a woman."

Brad nodded. "Distinction noted. What kind of a job?"

"Listen, I'd settle for just about anything! I've got to get out into the world more." She had a notion that she was about to start muttering recklessly. "That's what my ex-husband was always telling me, and do you know something? For once, he was right. I should have gotten a job the instant he walked out."

"What kind of job?" Brad persisted.

"I told you: anything. Within reason, that is."

"What's within reason?"

Carla blushed. "Well, you know. I mean, it has to be decent and everything."

"Oh," Brad said. "Sure, I thought maybe we were talking money."

"Money's not so important at this point in time," Carla said. "I'm not really trained for anything. I mean, I'm not a chemist or a computer programmer or lawyer or anything, so I couldn't expect to land a big and important job right off. I'm aware of that."

"Well," Brad said, "I happen to know of an opening. It's not very much, but it's something."

Carla reached over and touched the back of his hand with her fingertips. "Really? Are you kidding?"

Brad shook his head. "Nope. One of my laundromats. The woman just quit. She has to have an operation."

"A laundromat?"

"Well, you said it wouldn't have to pay much."

Carla thought a moment. This wasn't exactly what she had in mind, even though she hadn't really had anything *specific* in mind.

"You know," Brad said. "To tide you over."

Carla nodded vaguely. "Well, I suppose it might be all right. What would I have to do?"

"Just manage it, from eight to four. I got the four to midnight covered. You make change, even though there's an automatic bill changer—but you've got to keep it filled . . . and you keep the place clean. Also, you take stuff for dry cleaning, which a guy picks up twice a day and takes to our Madison Street office. One good thing, you don't have to dress up the way you would for an office job."

"I don't know," Carla said. "It doesn't sound very challenging."

"Nobody said it was," Brad said. "I didn't hear the word 'challenging' come up."

Carla nodded. "I know. But somehow . . ."

"I was just trying to help out," Brad said, taking the straw from behind his ear.

Something in his voice got her attention. "It's not that I'm not grateful or anything."

"Sure," he said. "I understand."

For a moment they were both silent, and then Carla surprised both of them—probably herself more than Brad—by blurting out: "But why not? Sure, I'll give it a try."

She knew she had to get out of the house, even though there'd been no mention of salary. Tim was driving her crazy with his quiet, studious ways, and at that instant she realized she hadn't really gone into details with Brad about Tim. She was confused, but certain.

Probably, Brad wouldn't have understood her anxiety at all. As she'd said to Rita over the phone once, it was hard to explain. And sensitivity wasn't Brad Lassiter's long suit, you could tell.

But the job turned out to be pretty awful. If Carla had thought the OASIS group was bad, what about the poor, drab, miscellaneous creatures who brought their dirty clothes into the laundromat and shoved them into the big washers and languidly pushed their quarters in the slots and then went over to sit in the plastic chairs and watch the TV set that was always tuned to the same dumb channel and was placed on a specially made shelf near the ceiling, too high for anybody to turn it off, even, let alone to another channel? As for this channel, it was game-show oriented, and the audio was pretty much limited to excited exclamations, canned laughter, and zippy musical cues . . . with an occasional answer to a question thrown in, just to keep up an honest appearance.

By the end of the first month, she told Tim that it was practically driving her crazy. She said she had never realized how much she hated television, especially when it was always on and you couldn't turn it off and couldn't stop watching it. What she didn't tell Tim was that with her new job she never saw Brad Lassiter at all; and every Wednesday, when the time for the OASIS meeting came around, she was just too tired to go. Assuming that Brad would show up, which she seriously doubted.

Thinking about this, she began to wonder if maybe Brad hadn't been sort of lying in wait for her, ready to pounce. Not *her*, specifically, but some desperate, lonely woman to take a job like this. Maybe that was the only reason he'd come to the OASIS meetings, to snare some woman gullible enough to be taken in by his sort-of-good looks. The thought made her squirm, until another idea came to her that was even worse. It was the idea that even though he'd never once touched her in an intimate way, he was nevertheless a secret lover who'd betrayed her, somehow. The fact that she didn't actually have any passionate and abandoned memories to regret made the idea of his betrayal all the worse.

And yet, she couldn't gather enough courage to quit. She knew that all she had to do was phone Brad and tell him how she felt. He'd even arranged to have her paychecks mailed to her every two weeks, as if he didn't want anything to do with her personally! And yet, she realized that if she quit, it would make her feel all the more foolish, somehow; it would be like admitting he'd cheated on her, in a way, and she'd made a mistake in trusting him. Which she had certainly done, but there was no point in admitting it, either to herself or others, especially with Brad Lassiter laughing up his sleeve with his warm beer breath. She wondered if he was still attending OASIS meetings, now that she herself was too tired to go out on Wednesday evenings after working eight hours.

The local newspaper had run a nice feature on the group, along with photos; but Brad wasn't mentioned, nor could she make him out in one of the photos of the meeting, although Gary Rickover was identifiable, sitting in the front row. Maybe she'd phone Wendy or somebody to find out; but the thought of doing that seemed degrading, somehow, so she decided not to lower herself by phoning any of them, even though she had a good excuse.

Then there was Tim's graduation from high school coming up, and she wanted to buy him something really special; and whatever gift she decided on, she wanted it to be paid for with her own money, not money from Jerry. She wanted the gift to be untainted, and there didn't seem to be any better way for her to earn it than with the job she had right now, working at Brad Lassiter's drab laundromat and wearing a green cotton apron with yellow fringe and making change and answering questions and keeping the place clean for the sort of people who wouldn't have noticed if moss was growing on the walls.

Then on the fourth Thursday after she'd taken her new job at Lassiter's laundromat, two things happened. Tim was notified that he'd been awarded a full-tuition scholarship at the state university, and Wendy Paulis phoned. Carla was naturally excited by the news, and told Wendy right away that her son had gotten a scholarship.

"Listen," Wendy said, "I think that's wonderful, but that's not the reason I called."

Carla thought that was a dopey thing to say—because how could she have known about it to call?—but she didn't say anything to Wendy. And she braced herself against the possibility that Brad's name might come up. There was something in Wendy's voice, she could tell. "What is it?" she asked.

"You have no idea how OASIS has taken off," Wendy said.

"It has?"

"Carla, it's grown by leaps and bounds."

"I haven't been there, so I wouldn't know."

"I know you haven't, and that's one reason I called. Do you know how many members we have now?"

"No. How many?"

"Thirty-nine regular, paid-up members."

Carla was impressed. "Why, that's over double!" she said.

"Don't I know it," Wendy said. "That newspaper feature story really got people interested. Did you read it?"

Carla said that she had.

"Only, everybody misses you," Wendy continued. "They've been asking where you are and everything."

"I've been working," Carla said.

"We all know that, but you don't work nights, so we wish you'd come back. Do you know something? We really miss you, the way you used to liven things up!"

For a moment Carla tried to remember how anybody could have said she'd livened things up. Mostly, she'd had the feeling that she just sort of sat there like a bump on a log while Wendy and the other talkers kept things moving. Dumb as a sled track, as her uncle from West Virginia used to say. Maybe she'd talked more than she'd realized. This was a possibility, of course, because people always tend to exaggerate how much other people talk and how little opportunity they themselves have to get a word in edgewise.

"And especially this next Wednesday," Wendy said.

"What about next Wednesday?"

"Well, like I was just saying, it's our second anniversary dinner. We've sent out invitations. Family members are invited, for those who have any. Or friends, of course. Didn't you get yours?"

"I'm not sure."

"Well, that's one reason I called. Listen, everybody wants you to be sure to show up, and I promised I'd get in touch with you. Carla, you can't let your old friends down!"

Carla almost asked, "*What* old friends?" but fortunately, she did not. Maybe they'd all been closer to one another than she'd realized.

"So do you promise?"

"Well," Carla said, "I guess so."

"That's good enough for me. And be sure to bring your son. He must be a grown man now, if he's got a scholarship for college. Listen, it just hasn't been the same without you, Carla!"

With that, Wendy hung up, and Carla stood there by the phone for a moment, her hand still resting on it, thinking about what Wendy had said. Was she sincere? Could it be true? Now, she'd have to go to the anniversary dinner to find out. And maybe she really would take Tim. She was certainly proud of him, in spite of everything. Obviously, a lot had changed at what Brad used to call "the old dry Oasis," and she was naturally curious.

She hadn't asked if Brad was planning to attend, although once or twice during their brief conversation, she'd thought of doing so; but somehow she couldn't just come out and ask Wendy. She wondered if Brad was still a member. He'd talked about quitting—she could remember every word. Or she wondered if, having been a member of OASIS long enough to find a woman dumb enough to take a job in one of his laundromats, he'd gone on to greener pastures.

Well, she'd find out next Wednesday. And she'd also be able to meet all of those new members. Thirty-nine! She could hardly believe it. She wondered if the 320-pound woman was still among them. She still couldn't remember her name.

It really was a nice occasion. They'd gone to a lot of trouble to convert the basement of St. James into a festive banquet hall. They had a vodka and pineapple juice punch, along with a speaker named Dr. Evelyn Brewster, who was a psychiatrist, family consultant, and authority on singles' life style. She had written a very successful book, titled *Learning to Live Alone, Not Lonely*, which all of the original members had read shortly after OASIS was formed.

The fat lady was not there, but Hal Hurst was there, with his Prince Val haircut dyed even blacker than Carla remembered. His complexion was yellow and wrinkled, and he looked awful. And Candi Thatcher was there, along with Patti Becker. Both seemed contented, but unnaturally reticent. And Ned was there, thin and round-shouldered in a green evening dress.

Also Brad Lassiter was there, along with his eighteen-year-old daughter, Melinda. Melinda Lassiter. The name struck Carla as being more than unfortunate—it almost sounded like some kind of goofy curse. Not only that, the poor girl didn't have any of Brad's features—she was almost as skinny as poor Ned; and she was too pale, although her heavily shadowed eyes were enormous. She wore a low-cut pink dress that was very unbecoming and revealed her bony shoulders. Brad was stiff and formal when they all introduced themselves, and Carla noticed that Tim hardly looked at the girl. That worried her a little—the boy was miles away, you could tell.

"Didn't I tell you we were growing by leaps and bounds?" Wendy Paulis said from behind, surprising Carla and making her jump. Wendy was holding a glass of punch in one hand and a cigarello in the other as she moved in front and beamed at her.

Wendy pointed her cigarello at Carla's glass. "Listen, watch out for that stuff; it's dynamite." Carla looked down at it, vaguely aware that she was already on her second one.

Wendy touched her arm with her fingertips. There was something almost pleading in the gesture. "Didn't I tell you how much we'd grown?" she asked again, obviously anxious for Carla to answer, as if her opinion were charged with mysterious authority.

Brad mumbled something and ran his hand through his hair, and Carla said, "Well, there certainly are some new faces!" She looked around and noticed that the men were still outnumbered three or four to one, but she didn't say anything.

"Listen, Carla," Wendy said, "we've really missed you, and do you know something?"

Wary, Carla asked what.

"Several of us were wondering if you would be willing to accept a nomination for president."

For a moment, Carla felt unsteady on her feet. The question actually made her woozy. President of OASIS? My God, what would they think of next? Had they really been talking about her during her absence when she felt so much on the edge of things? Had they really *missed* her?

"This is my son," she said, presenting Tim as a distraction so she could gather her thoughts. "You know, the one with the scholarship."

"How wonderful," Wendy said, shaking Tim's hand.

It really was impressive how fast the group had grown. And to think that all this time—when she'd been away and everything—her reputation had somehow not only been kept alive, but had been *secretly growing with them!*

"How about it?" Wendy asked. She certainly was persistent. Carla had forgotten how persistent she was.

"Well," she said, pausing to sip her punch as she cast her eyes ceiling-ward, "I'll have to think about it."

"To me," Wendy said happily, "that always means just one thing: y-e-s, yes."

Blurred, Carla half-turned and stared at all the people. Brad acted at loose ends. He didn't have a drink in his hand and seemed to have drifted a little farther away. She was suddenly aware that several minutes had passed without her noticing. Everybody was talking boisterously, having a great time.

She felt hot and heavy, almost the way she'd felt right before her period back in the bad old menstrual days. Maybe she was just feeling her drinks. Suddenly, she realized that it wasn't her at all— the room was overheated. And Wendy had wandered off, not to mention Brad and Melinda and Tim. She looked down at her glass of punch and saw that it had gotten empty again.

Then someone tapped a spoon against a water glass and announced that dinner would soon be served and they should all take their seats behind the place names set out for them. There was a general feeling of gaiety while everybody bustled about and found their places and settled down. Soon they were served hearty portions of roast chicken breast (which Hal referred to as "chicken bosoms," thinking he was being very funny), fresh peas, baked potatoes, and rolls with sesame seed. Somebody sneezed; she thought it was a man and had to maintain self-control in order not to turn and look.

After a cherry cobbler dessert, the business meeting was held. Carla's armpits felt hot and damp. She didn't remember knowing about any of this. She'd thought it was just an anniversary banquet. Everything seemed strange to her. She wouldn't have recognized the old basement of St. James, where they'd once had such interesting discussions. When the election for a new president was held, Carla's name was the only one submitted, and she was unanimously approved and elected. Somehow, she felt like an ugly old princess.

It had all happened as if her fate had been decided long ago. Think of what happens when you stay away! She'd become someone important, whereas if she'd shown up for meetings faithfully, the way she had once done, they might have taken her for granted, and nobody would have paid the slightest attention to her. Could this be right?

A woman named Trisha Kellogg was elected secretary-treasurer. Then Ms. Brewster, the evening's speaker, was introduced by Patti Becker, who'd been strangely quiet all evening. (Was it possible that *she* had wanted to be elected president?) Ms. Brewster took her place behind the podium and fussed with the microphone before starting to speak in a shy, trembling, husky, faraway soprano.

Carla sat there blurred and smiling throughout the talk by Ms. Brewster. Although their guest speaker seemed to talk a long time, by the time she'd finished, Carla couldn't remember a thing she'd said. Still, she applauded as loudly as anyone when Ms. Brewster—who was obviously wearing a brown wig—sat down.

Everyone came up and congratulated Carla afterwards. And, once, when a woman with a lot of eyeshadow and a black Spanish shawl asked her a question about her future plans for OASIS, she looked over the woman's shoulder and was surprised to see Tim and Brad Lassiter's daughter talking together. What was her name? Melinda.

She didn't know where Brad was. Probably drunk, somewhere; or maybe out tracking down some dumb woman to come work for him. Trisha Kellogg came up and introduced herself, and Carla assured her, sounding very confident and authoritative, that the two of them could work together. It seemed to be the appropriate thing to say, even if Carla couldn't have had any idea whether they could work together or not. Still she supposed that was the way politicians had to talk. It created the proper condition for success—maybe what Tim would call a self-fulfilling prophecy, which he said was always more or less functional in the stock market.

But whatever the wisdom behind it, she had said it without hesitation or even thought. It just seemed perfectly natural. Maybe there was a secret wisdom in all of them electing her president—a wisdom that none of them were aware of. Maybe she'd be transformed from a nobody into a powerful and effective leader, like what they said about Harry Truman.

She pondered these ideas, and then took a deep breath and looked around. These were her people, now, in a way that she couldn't have conceived before. Also, she was theirs. A thrill went through her at the notion, and she forced herself to think of Trisha Kellogg, who seemed like a nice young woman, even though she was too heavy and had buck teeth and her dark red hair was puffed out in a way that was scarcely complimentary.

She couldn't help looking for Brad; apparently he'd taken off. There was quite a crowd, but he wasn't among them. He was gone.

Who would take his daughter home? No sooner had the question occurred to her than she saw Melinda being escorted out the door by two women, one of whose names was McNulty, or something like that.

What a crowd of strangers, and now she was their president!

All the way home she held in her astonishment in the way you keep from throwing up when you're nauseated. Tim was driving and didn't say a word. He might have thought that she had known all about it, but little did he know! And yet, *she* had noticed something; she had noticed how Tim and Brad's daughter seemed to be getting along with each other.

After while, Carla swallowed and said, "Melinda certainly does seem to be a nice girl."

Without nodding, Tim nodded.

Shocked, she thought about the expression on his face, which her sideways glance had detected. She knew his nods, some of which were more eloquent than whole speeches; and this was one of them. Tim was actually *attracted* to her! What would Brad ever think of that?

When they arrived home, Carla trudged upstairs to bed, still dense with the evening's events. She was now the president of OASIS, and there was nothing she could do about it. The group seemed entirely different to her. Better, somehow; more important. Of course she understood that part of this apparent change might well be from the perspective of her own vanity—she wasn't about to fool herself. But there was something more than that—the way a building looks different from inside than it does from without.

Then it all came to her in a rush: Tim and Melinda would get married. She had a premonition. Something about it struck her as inevitable. Maybe some of her conviction derived from all the punch she'd drunk, but she wasn't really *that* drunk!

She told herself she should be glad that Tim was showing interest in a nice young girl. It was about time, because the fact was, she'd been a little worried about him, growing up without a male role model around the house for the past three or four all-important years. And there had been times when she'd even wondered if maybe he might not have a slight tendency to be homosexual.

But now she was confident such fears had not been justified. Tim had really been attracted to Melinda Lassiter, you could tell. Carla began to feel a little bit sick at her stomach again and wondered why something like this couldn't have happened to *her*. What was wrong with Brad? Why hadn't he kept in touch? All she did was work for him, and at a salary that was insulting, when you thought about it. Was it really possible that he'd only been using her? Was it possible that the only reason he'd taken her to that Wendy's, even, was not because he was attracted to her as a woman, but just because he needed to find somebody who could take over one of his laundromats?

When she pulled her dress up over her head, she realized that not one person had said she'd looked nice all evening. She had told at least four of them they looked nice. Maybe five. Thinking about this was like looking down a dark hold, so she turned her thoughts away from it. What was wrong with her, anyway? And why couldn't she say no? What did it matter to be president of a wacky group like OASIS? And what about Tim? What was a child to a woman, after all? And, speaking of that, what was a man, and what on earth was a woman to do with them, anyway?

THE STOLEN HARP

It is hardly surprising that
the realm of the Giants is so remote from us, and so inconceivable.
Indifferent to our ignorance, however, it lasts on—vaporous, majestic,
silent, in a time measured by alien clocks.

Nor is it to be wondered at that the Giants have shown so little
interest in communicating with us. This is chiefly due to a single
outrageous and infamous fable, whose moral focus is so warped and
clearly wrong that it is a miracle that even so gullible and self-satisfied
a race as ourselves could ever fail to turn away from it in disgust and
loathing. Even as children, we should know better. At least, this is
how the Giants view the matter, and it is no doubt one reason for
their silence and mysterious invisibility.

The story I am speaking of is known to everyone. It is known
by several names and in several versions: but all of them share the
central narrative of a wretched and cowardly little boy who invades
the realm of the Giants through the intercession of magic and commits
three crimes in addition to trespass: theft, kidnapping, and homicide.
No doubt these charges come as a surprise to most people, which only
shows how depraved and undeveloped our powers of detection are,
and how ill-fitted for reality. But it is all there in the story as we have
known it since we were children. It is there for all of us to see, if we
will only look.

In no version is the Giant named, but of course he had a name, Bildigal (accented equally on the first and last syllables, as in *madrigal*). He was not ageless—as most of us suppose Giants to be in Fairyland—but of a specific age: he was 47 years old. And his dimensions are as well known as if he'd been issued a driver's license: he was 24 feet 7 inches tall and weighed (in terms of the earth's gravity) 3976 pounds. To some that might seem exceedingly heavy, but such people fail to take into consideration the disproportionate increase of mass over volume: Bildigal was actually a lean, even skinny, Giant, and he walked with one shoulder higher than the other.

Bildigal was a retired gardener, which is an occupation of great honor among Giants, since its labors are all consonant with the music made by water, clay, and mold. That Bildigal was married is testified in all the familiar versions, but it is seldom implied that this marriage was quite a happy one, even though such is known to be the case. Bildigal's wife, Tru-ewd, was a nervous, anxious woman, scarcely seventeen feet tall. She had moles all over her forehead and left breast, which caused her to live her life in a nimbus of half-hearted shame, for the Giants are extremely sensitive concerning their personal appearance.

In the realm of the Giants they have always told stories about little people. For generations such tales have been handed down, and like our fairy tales, they are formulaic, simple, and marvelous. All of them picture forth a small, dense world wherein creatures very like the Giants themselves—though no larger than cats or spaniels—live and quarrel and muddle their way through whole sagas of petty yearnings and grandiose deceit.

It is understood, however, that the stories they tell are only a small sampling of the Little People—too prolonged a narrative (they say) would likely depress, even vitiate, the common morality.

"Why do they behave that way?" their children sometimes ask; and the answer is always the same: "They are small, and that is why they resort to deceit and trickery. If they were as large as peach trees, they would not act in such a way."

"They're smaller than *peach trees?*" the children ask wonderingly, their imaginations pricked.

And their parents nod and smile, as human parents do when they speak of Santa Claus in response to the questions of a four-year old.

But one might ask: since all the Giants are generally of the same size, wouldn't they themselves be subjected to envy, resentment, and distrust just as we are? Wouldn't their relative vastness be irrelevant in view of the fact that within their sphere some would be larger and stronger (and yes, more clever) than others?

But the answer to this has already been given, in effect: all other objects in their world (other than their pets and domestic animals) were of the same magnitude as they are in ours, so that a Giant seldom came upon a tree that was more than four or five times his own height. A giant oak or redwood was to Bildigal no taller than an elm sapling or dogwood would be to us. Thus, they have this moral injunction: "Hug one another with tenderness, the way you carry a tree to be transplanted, knowing that we, too, can be uprooted into the air and die."

So far as is known, that infamous invasion by the clever and agile boy is the only human invasion of the Giant's realm. The reason for this is complex and ill understood, although some say that is because the realm of the Giants is not fixed overhead, like some primitive notion of Heaven, but is instead slanted backwards in time.

Thus, in the realm of the Giants, time happens one-half second after it happens in the world we live in. Their realm, it may be said, occupies ours an instant after all that we know has vacated that slice of time we call "The Present."

In view of this fact, the magic beans not only sprouted with supernatural swiftness, but they grew backwards in time, so that in climbing it, the world the meddlesome boy had always known faded into the nothingness of the immediate future, always half a step beyond.

No one could possibly ever understand such a thing, of course; but it might be true, anyway, because as anyone can see, there is no realm of the Giants overhead, and it is inconceivable that there has ever been such a realm.

Since the events of the story are so well known, there will be no point in going over each and every detail. You know about the mother's desperation; her sending her little boy out to sell the cow; his trading the cow for a handful of beans; his return home; his angry mother's exasperated response; and her throwing the seemingly useless beans out the window, where they took root and grew overnight into a great shaggy green ladder of a beanstalk that reached upward so far they could not see the top.

This was the real, living, growing plant by which Jack ascended into the unreal domain of the Giants. As he climbed, the air got darker all about him, and it was like coming into a rain cloud. And then it got lighter again, and he could see the beginnings of some kind of earth all around him, as if the beanstalk was inside a sort of well or mine shaft, narrowing as it rose toward a goblet of light.

And then, finally, he emerged through the opening—walled in stone like a great well—and stepped out upon another ground. Here he felt much lighter than he had upon the real earth, which made him wonder if he might not be dreaming. This lesser gravity is characteristic of that other realm, and enables the Giants to grow so large, for if they were subjected to the earth's gravity they would be pulled at with nightmarish power, and the least fall would smash their limbs and bodies, and the density of air would suffocate them.

As for Jack, he was as lively as a cricket, and he jumped thirty feet in the air and landed as softly as a sparrow on a limb or an empty glove thrown onto a bed. When a great house cat—six feet tall—came up to him, he easily outraced her, darting like a ferret into some weeds, and shot away.

No wonder he was excited; he felt full of tricks and unfocused liveliness—which is what his name signified at that time. He ran swift as a mouse, jumped over tree limbs as thick as a man's waist, and whistled and yelled in the pale mountainous air.

But after a while, he calmed down enough to look around, and made his way through some high grass at the edge of the little copse he was in.

There he saw something which made him catch his breath. It was a vast and majestic castle, lofty and vague as a cloud. It did not cast a shadow, so that it seemed to be made out of sunlight and air, and was, he suspected, no weightier, in all its voluminous looming, than a bushel of dead leaves.

All stories are meant to conceal even as they reveal themselves. They are told in various sorts of code, and it is our business to solve them in all their implications. The fact that Bildigal's name was never mentioned, for example, is significant; it is evidence of an evasion, a refusal to acknowledge the Giant's reality, if not his humanity. And the fact that it is Jack himself who is the only character named in the story permeates all that we know about it; and this fact, unlike

77

Bildigal's great, mountainous castle, faceted with sunlight . . . this fact does in truth suffuse all that happens.

The story is rooted deep in the life of the language. By the time it was first intoned in ignorance and secret cunning, Jack was known to be the essence of knaves. He had taken his place in the pack of cards, the machinery of chance and cunning.

Furthermore, Jack was of the common people, *vulgaris*, often associated with the old Irish servant girl, whose title was "Gill" (as in the surname Gilpatrick, or Kilpatrick, "servant of St. Patrick"); and of course, "Jack and Gill" was changed, under the pressure of alliteration, to "Jack and Jill," which presents another event in the life of this lowly trickster, in which he, like Icarus, climbs higher than he ought and suffers for it—the lowly, insolent, adolescent trickster tricked.

Then there are all those other base connections; the male animal, stubborn and intractable, cunning in its insolent refusal to be trained, the jackass. But this is only one of a whole population, which includes the jackdaw, jackfish, jack kestrel, jack salmon, jack crow, jack-in-a-bottle (a male titmouse), and finally, jack spaniard, which is a kind of wasp found in the Carib Isles.

But most interesting and telling is the name's reference to a clever dwarf or subtle old child, whose presence in folklore lasts on only in two dimensions of thinness, which is to say, Jack Sprat.

It was a sly boy of this sort, then—meddlesome, cocky, shrewd, vulgar, and unprincipled—who first invaded the Giant's realm, where he stole a bag of gold from Bildigal, himself a humble, unobtrusive, and otherwise unremarkable creature.

On his second ascent of the beanstalk, it will be recalled, our tawdry and hyperactive hero stole Bildigal's hen that laid golden eggs. Like the loss of his bag of gold (only one of many), this was not in itself enough to trouble Bildigal overmuch. Though he was ignorant, even for a Giant, Bildigal was wise in his way, and had little use for gold. He preferred real omelets—dotted with mushrooms and onion crescents, with long, rubbery, yellow threads of cheese woven into them— to the clank of gold coins. Bildigal did not have the insidious gift for abstraction or poetry, either one, that could fire his heart with the thought of wealth.

But it was on this trip that Bildigal first suspected Jack's presence, so that while the brat was still there hiding behind the breadbox, the Giant said to his wife: "Tru-ewd, hast ever thought there might be little folk about?"

Now as you know from the story, the Giant's wife had already encountered the boy, and had talked with him. Furthermore, she had demonstrated a certain sympathy toward him, along with a fear of her husband. But this was in the versions you have read, in which neither Bildigal nor Tru-ewd has a name: and how much truth can you expect from such an account as that, which does not even acknowledge the named-ness of such poor creatures as Giants?

Actually, though Tru-ewd suffered from various anxieties, she was basically a good and loyal wife. Her chief anxiety had to do with housekeeping, for she was extremely fastidious; thus it was that when she first encountered Jack, whom she'd surprised near the hen, she grabbed him. He squirmed like a strong little rat and bit her finger, so that she had to drop him. For an instant, the two stood and stared at each other in astonishment; and then she shooed him into a cupboard, for the sound of Bildigal's footsteps came to her ears.

In all this there was not a word spoken, and the fact is, there would have been no communication if there had been, for the language of the Giants is quite different from any human language.

When Bildigal came into the kitchen, Jack scampered from the cupboard up onto the counter and then behind the breadbox—once again marveling at how quick and powerful he had become in the low gravitational field of this strange place where he found himself.

When he'd darted behind the breadbox, Bildigal might have caught a glimpse of him, just the flick of his passing, as when you see a mouse dart across the room at the edge of your vision. It was at this time that Bildigal asked his wife: "Hast ever thought there might be little folk about?"

Poor Tru-ewd trembled to her knees, turned pale, and didn't answer for a moment, finally clutching her hand at the lace on her bosom as if to steady herself. "No," she whispered. "I've never thought such a thing, Bildigal."

Her husband nodded (Jack saw it all): "But I hear things," he muttered. "I hear scampering and scratching and feel the thud of small bodies on the floor and imagine that there is a flickering in the air."

Tru-ewd said nothing to this, but attended to her work in the kitchen, mixing the batter for a great mutton pie in a pan big enough for Jack to sit in.

It was this last utterance of the Giant that has been grossly and in truth libelously translated as the famous:

Fee, Fie, Fo, Fum,
I smell the blood of an Englishman'
Be he alive or be he dead,
I'll grind his bones to make my bread!

It is on his third trip that the boy's villainy is fully exposed. Conversely, the simple-hearted innocence of the Giant is revealed, along with the tragic ending that all of us, from our low perspective, interpret as joyous and triumphant.

For in every version of the tale, Jack's third and last trick is his stealing of the harp, which was a living creature. Jack himself heard the terrified harp call out: "Master! Master!"

Here, the coincidence is strange almost beyond belief: for in the language of the Giants the word for "master" is the very same as ours—an accident that does not necessarily occur even once in two different languages, in spite of thousands of words they contain, for we all know that different languages are not made up of the same sounds, as if they were musical notes; but are made up of sounds that are in themselves radically different.

Perhaps Jack was able to interpret the plaintive call of the harp. Surely, even that selfish and insensitive little ruffian could detect the pain and yearning in the harp's cry. But of course, busy on his own behalf, he cared nothing for the feelings of another.

Nor would he have cared if he had known of the ancient custom among the Giants to raise their musical instruments as children. It is well known that harps are little girls, and it was with the terror of a young girl being abducted that the harp called out to Bildigal . . . as if to a father, to save her from being dragged down into hell.

This is what that hole led to, of course: there was no Lake Avernus surrounding it, but there was no doubt as to where it would take one if ever a Giant tried to descend.

It was said that several curious and adventurous Giants in past centuries had climbed down the inner walls. They had descended with great ropes, as mountain climbers do, or spelunkers. But they had all returned with the same report of feeling the density and darkness beginning to smother them . . . so that the farther they descended, the greater the danger became that they would plummet all the way into that measureless darkness of the instantaneous Future, which is another name for hell among the Giants.

The scruffy, energetic urchin who stole Bildigal's harp killed the poor Giant only indirectly, in that he forced him into suicide. Because the Giant was not trying to catch the boy, he was only trying to retrieve his harp.

His reason for this would be immediately understood by the Giants, but has been strongly ignored by human creatures: Bildigal threw himself into the abyss because he could not endure the thought of living in a world without music.

Tru-ewd told his story over and over again, until she died—a poor, mad, twisted, love-starved old woman.

But the children who heard her tell it never forgot. And it is they who have handed the story, scarcely altered in the least detail, down through those generations of Giants who live so near and yet so far away.

RECURRING DREAMS

One day my grandfather went into town to buy some more fertilizer, and my grandmother went with him to shop, leaving me all alone on the farm. I had told them I didn't want to go with them.

Before they left, Grandpa said, "Now don't you bother old Hector, do you hear? Just stay away from the barn and you'll be all right. He figures the barnyard is his territory, so just stay out of his range. Don't go back any farther than the henhouse. He'll stay in his place, and you stay in yours. Do you hear?"

I told him I did and he nodded. "I'm sure if you leave old Hector alone, he won't bother you. And the thing is, we have to respect him: he's too old to change his ways."

"They say you can't teach an old dog new tricks," Grandma said, punching me on the arm with her fist and grinning. "God knows that's true of your Grandpa. Are you *sure* you don't want to go to town with us?"

"No, I like it here just fine."

"So do I, but that doesn't mean I don't like to go to town, now and then."

"I thought you liked to come with me to the old feed store," Grandpa said, shoving his hands in his pockets and half-smiling down at me.

"I just want to stay here, if it's okay."

"Sure, it's *okay*," Grandpa said. "Do you think I'm going to keep a grown-up farm hand like you away from work? Why, maybe you can go out there and hoe some more sweet corn in the garden. Do you suppose?"

"I guess so."

"Do you think we should really leave him here all alone?" Grandma asked him.

Grandpa laughed. "Why, sure! What's so bad about being all alone out here on the old place? He can hoe that sweet corn. Our pal here is a good farm hand, that's the way I look at it."

"But he's still so young!"

"Why, no, he's a big boy now, aren't you?"

I nodded.

Grandma wasn't so sure, however, and she hemmed and hawed and said she wondered if we were doing the right thing; but Grandpa repeated that I was a big boy, now, and it wasn't as if they were going to Australia or some place.

She nodded, and then they got in their old gray and black Oldsmobile and drove off down the road toward town, leaving a cloud of dust behind them, until it drifted away in the hot wind.

When they were almost out of sight, a Carolina wren started singing in the maple tree, which was so close I almost jumped at the sound. All that noise coming out of such a little instrument, the way Grandma had said one time.

I remember standing in the backyard, hearing the hens clucking as they strutted all around, pecking at grubs in the dry sod; and then I watched the paddlewheel of the windmill next to the near shed as it turned slowly in the dry wind. Up close, you could hear it squeak when it turned.

Then I looked way out back past the shed and the chicken house, and saw Hector lying in the long grass on the cool and shady side of the barn. His tan head was raised as he stared back at me, and even from that distance, I could imagine his wet nose quivering as he tried to pick up my scent. He would do that when Grandpa was near and Hector always behaved himself, so that we could all be close to him and not think anything about it.

I wondered how near I could approach the barn before Hector would stand up and start trotting toward me, treacherously wagging his tail. There was a time when I had thought that whenever a dog wagged its tail, it was being friendly; but that was before I'd gotten to know Hector.

Already, the morning was hot. The clucking of the hens was a lonely sound, and the whirring of the hot dry breeze made me feel even lonelier. I went over to the windmill and listened to the paddlewheel squeak for a while, but then it suddenly stopped, and I realized the breeze had stopped, too, and everything was quiet and hot, except for the sound of a car on the road, only it was over the hill and far away.

I went back inside the house, where it was cool, and I walked through the kitchen, and then the pantry, and into the front room. The stained cherry clock was ticking away on the wall, with its pendulum wagging back and forth. I thought of how Hector wagged his tail, pretending to be friendly, but only fooling you, because he would bite the instant you looked away or did the least thing he didn't approve of, like letting your shadow fall over his worthless tan hide or yellow eyes.

He was a good-for-nothing beast, surely; even Grandpa would say that about him, using those very words. Sometimes Grandpa would say it even when he was grabbing the loose hide around Hector's neck and shaking him so hard that specks of saliva would fly off of Hector's wagging tongue.

I thought of the way his tongue would wag when Grandpa shook him that way, then I thought of the way Hector would wag his tail when he would come trotting toward you, if you got too near the barn, and then I thought of the pendulum wagging underneath the clock on the wall. Wagging, wagging, wagging.

And then I thought of Grandpa's .22 rifle upstairs in the hall closet.

The clock said it was almost 10:30, and I was looking out the window at the dusty road that went to town. The milk truck had come about ten minutes ago, and the man had backed it up to Grandpa's loading ramp next to the road, and I watched him get out and roll the big milk cans to the back of his truck and lift them over onto the truck bed, making the hood of his little truck nod, like it knew the feel of an extra milk can and it was all right.

I stood there beside the loading ramp and watched, and the milkman asked where Grandpa and Grandma were, and I said they were in town.

He was a big fat man, and wore glasses and a gray T-shirt that was dark and wet under the armpits, where he was sweating. He said, "That's right, he told me he had to get some more fertilizer, and I told him I didn't think the price would get any better, so he said he thought he'd go in today and get some."

"Grandma went with him," I said.

The milkman laughed. "So that means you're all alone, does it? You're the man of the house today, is that right?"

I told him it would just be for this morning.

"Yes, I don't guess the old lady would let it come lunchtime, with you here alone and nothing for your belly."

I nodded and told him she'd said they'd be back in time so she could fix my lunch.

"She's one fine old lady, that one is," the milkman said, shaking his head. Everybody seemed to like Grandma and Grandpa. "And you're a big boy to be able to stay here all alone with them in town. How's come they didn't take you?"

"I wanted to stay here."

"A boy your age, and you wanted to stay here all alone? And they let you? Now, aren't you the big boy, though."

"Sometimes," I said.

He laughed. "Like this morning, right?"

"Maybe," I said.

"Sure do need that rain, don't we?"

"Sure do," I told him.

The clock struck 10:30, so I made up my mind and went upstairs.

I went to the closet and opened the door, and the smell of mothballs came out. My mouth was dry, and my heart was beating fast. I reached around some coats and felt the cool metal barrel of the .22, leaning there in the closet, right where I knew Grandpa kept it.

I knew this because of how often he had told the story about how he'd killed the skunk that had been getting to his chickens; and he always laughed when he told how he'd aimed for its damned little head and he'd killed that skunk with his first shot . . . but the skunk had polluted the entire county with its expiring breath.

This was exactly the way he put it, because I can remember hearing him tell the story time again, and remember how he loved to say the words slowly: "polluted the entire county with its expiring breath."

I put three of the .22 long rifle cartridges in the chamber, the way I'd seen Grandpa do it when we'd gone target shooting together; and then I worked the bolt, injecting one of them into firing position. Grandpa had taught me how to use the gun, so I was confident that I was doing everything right.

The safety was automatically on, now; but I checked it anyway, and saw that it was exactly as it should be. Then I went downstairs and back through the pantry and the kitchen, and on to the back porch. I walked out the door, letting the loose screen slap shut behind me, and took ten or twelve steps out into the backyard before stopping.

Hector raised his head and stared at me from where he was lying down in the cool shadow of the barn. He was about a hundred yards away. If I had been a good shot, I might have been able to kill him from this distance, but I knew I couldn't be sure of my aim when he was so far away.

So I took another twenty or thirty steps, until I was even with the chicken house. The hens were all about, clucking and clucking, and I stood there, thinking. They wouldn't be back for almost an hour. Grandma had said they had a lot to do, and it would be at least 12:15 before they could get back; and she'd asked if I'd mind waiting for my lunch, and I'd said, no, that would be all right.

Now, I realized that it still wasn't too late to back out. I could take the rifle back into the house and upstairs and unload it and put the cartridges back in the dresser and put the rifle back in the hall closet. Nobody would know the difference.

The hens clucked and pranced all around me, and then I saw the rooster, who was cropping next to the fence on the other side of the hen house. I listened through their clucking, trying to hear the paddlewheel of the windmill squeak, and once I thought I heard it, but then the wind quieted down and there was only the sound of the clucking. The milk cows had been let out into the back pasture, and you could hardly ever hear them mooing, except maybe toward evening if they were late being milked.

Hector was still lying there in the shade watching me.

I stood there with the gun in my hands, looking back at him. I wondered if I could have hit him on the move if he'd started trotting toward me with his tail wagging. I thought of how he looked when he did that, and how it made you feel it all the way down inside your stomach, the way he was busily trotting toward you, wagging his tail, and yet you knew you couldn't trust him for a minute, for he had bitten two farm workers—one on the forearm, and taking the little finger off the other one, a man who was part-black, part Indian, and part-white. Everybody called him Pepper, which struck me as funny, since he was a quiet, easy going man, with sleepy eyes. But maybe that was his name. Anyway, Grandpa said he'd had the devil of a time keeping from being sued; but he'd managed to settle everything and keep old Hector, who he said was a sure-enough good-for-nothing beast and ought to be put out of his misery, if there was any justice in the world.

"You mean, put out of everybody *else's* misery," Grandma said; and Grandpa laughed and nodded and said, yep, that was just about one-hundred percent right.

Four steps beyond the chicken house, and Hector's head was held back a little. I'd seen him do this before. You couldn't trust it, any more than that wagging tail; for if he held his head back, he was getting ready to stand up and start trotting in your direction, his tail wagging like his tongue when it was hot and Grandpa was grabbing him by his loose neck skin and shaking his head, so that specks of saliva flew off his tongue and his yellow eyes looked sleepy and contented.

I took another step, Hector stood up and shook himself. His nose and yellow eyes were pointed at me as fixed as if they had been the sights of a rifle.

Then I think I heard him growl, and the sound was like somebody had a big fork and was stirring it deep down in my stomach.

My hands were sweaty and my mouth was dry. I could hear myself breathing hard, but behind that, I could hear the chickens clucking all around me; and behind those sounds, I was sure I could hear Hector growl so deep down that the sound was transmitted to me through the ground and the soles of my shoes.

By now I figured I'd gotten close enough. I didn't think I could take another step, so I stayed right where I was, holding the rifle halfway in position, so that if Hector started trotting toward me, I could lift it up and shoot.

But he didn't move; he just stood there, staring at me. Maybe he was suspicious of the rifle. It was something new, so far as he was concerned. At least it was something new for him to see me carrying it, instead of Grandpa.

I tried to judge the distance, but it was hard. Maybe sixty or seventy feet. I had gotten closer than Grandpa had said I should come. I had gone quite a distance beyond the henhouse, although the hens were still all around me, clucking and stepping high and pecking at grubs and other invisible things in the hot, dry sod. It was said that chickens got more protein from such foraging than from regular feed; Grandpa had often talked about this over supper, and Grandma had listened, nodding and not arguing with him.

Grandpa had taught me to get down on one knee when I was shooting in an open place and had a stationary target. He said that if I got down on my right knee and rested my left elbow on my left knee, I would have much more stability. He had taught me how to shoot, and I was confident I could hit a big target, especially one as big as Hector when I was this close.

In a way, I was surprised that he hadn't already started trotting toward me, wagging his tail. If a dog can be said to have an expression on his face, I thought that Hector might have been revealing a certain perplexity. He wasn't sure of what I was up to. Maybe, if I hadn't had the gun, he would have already started trotting toward me with that terrible wagging of the tail and those yellow eyes not blinking at all, but looking through you, as if you didn't exist, but you were going to have to be attacked anyway, and his teeth would clamp onto your arms and his heavy neck would start shaking you all over, and he was snarling all the time, and your arm was being crushed, and blood was dripping down over your hand, and you were trying to lurch away from him, screaming as hard as you could.

Slowly, I got down on my right knee, and Hector took three or four cautious steps toward me, and then stopped. I settled my left elbow onto my left knee and closed my left eye, then peered through the open sight of the .22 rifle and saw Hector's head come into the fork, the vee of the sight right between his yellow eyes.

Then I held my breath and gently squeezed the trigger, just as Grandpa had told me, and the gun went *pang*, and all the chickens broke out into a clucking that was so loud it was almost like a great thundercloud that has suddenly broken, and the first deep, powerful roll of thunder accumulates far in the distance, and then gathers momentum until it rumbles over the pale dry pastures, the woods beyond, and the dusty dirt road that leads into town.

I remember that terrible hurriedness, and throwing the gun down in the grass after I was sure he was dead; I remember running for the spade that was stuck at an angle in the garden; then I remember stopping and panting and whispering to myself, "Wait a minute!"

I went back and got Hector's body and started to drag it through the long grass. My God, it was heavy and limp! I stopped a moment to catch my breath, and then I dragged it up to the fence gate that led into the vegetable garden. I stopped and opened the gate and dragged Hector's body into the garden and down past the even rows of green onions, tomatoes, sweet potatoes, and cabbages to the sweet corn, that stood as tall as Grandpa, sighing in the dry wind.

There was the spade, sticking at an angle in the dirt. I pulled it out and began to dig a hole between the two rows of corn, digging as fast as I could, and panting as I stabbed the spade into the deep dark soil and lifted spadeful after spadeful up into growing piles of earth on both sides.

Once, I heard a car on the road, and I paused and listened until it passed; but long after it was beyond hearing, the pounding of my heart fluttered my shirt, and I kept swallowing saliva and gulping air.

I was shoveling again, going down and down in the soft earth—remembering how Grandpa had bragged that this had been a pigpen, once, and was the richest soil anywhere—going deeper and deeper, shoveling and panting, and between the sounds of the spade and my panting, hearing the far-off clucking of the chickens.

Several times, I thought of how easily Hector had died, just folding in on himself and then lifting one leg, as if he were about to pee at the sky, and letting it tremble for a minute, while I crept closer and closer to watch him die, still holding the .22 rifle ready, in case he wasn't dead yet. There was a neat hole just below his right eye, and blood seeped out of it while I watched. His yellow eyes were half-open and his lips were pulled back a little in a growling expression, showing his teeth ringed with blood.

Another car passed by, and I thought I was going to die of fright. Then, when I was three or four feet deep, I turned around and dragged Hector's limp body over the pile of dirt I'd made toward the hole I was standing in. It was hard to believe how heavy his body was, and how limp. I could see it ripple as I pulled it over the lumps of earth, and then it tumbled into the hole where I was standing, and pinned my feet in with its weight.

Panic flashed through me when that happened, and I scrambled and scrambled, until somehow I got up out of the hole, making Hector's lifeless head bob up and down while I was scrambling, as if his bloody death grin meant he'd known all along what was going to happen and it was all kind of funny.

Swiftly, I shoveled the dirt back into the hole, covering his body quickly, but leaving a mound of dirt in the corn row when I'd finished. I tramped it as flat as I could, then spread the dirt up and down, and even into the next row, after which I stabbed the space all over, to darken the soil and make it look like it might have been weeded.

Still another car passed, and I stood there motionless with my heart racing, whispering rapidly, "It isn't time yet, it isn't time yet!"

When I had leveled off the soil pretty well, I took the spade and went looking for blood where I had dragged Hector's body. I found several places, and turned the soil over so that the blood wouldn't show. Then I went through the gate, back into the barnyard, and found several blades of grass with blood on them, and pulled them and took them to the fence beyond the vegetable garden, and threw them out into the pasture.

Then I wiped my hands off on the grass as well as I could and ran back to the .22 rifle lying there where I'd dropped it, and picked it up and started running toward the house.

The screen door slammed behind me, and I ran upstairs, panting so hard I didn't think I could breathe. I stopped in the bathroom and washed my hands and looked all over for blood on my clothes, but I didn't see any.

Then I took the .22 into the hallway and ejected the cartridges back into their bedroom and put them with the others in the top right drawer.

I went downstairs, trying to think of anything I might have forgotten; but my mind was a blur; and then I went outside and wandered around, thinking that I was looking for spots of blood, but really not going back far enough, and just sort of walking around and listening to the chickens and the squeak of the paddlewheel on the windmill.

I kept thinking about how much we needed rain. That's all people seemed to talk about. Everybody said we needed it, but right at that moment, I was sure I wanted it more than anybody. I could almost feel the wetness on my skin, and the splashing of drops in the ruts in the barnyard, and the way it would turn all the soil in the garden dark, making it look pretty much the same all over.

But the sky was clear, and the hot breeze just kept blowing over me, while the wheel squeaked and the chickens clucked, and I knew that the clock hands in the front room had moved past twelve o'clock; and before long, I'd see another cloud of dust on the road, and this time, it would be them, and they would be coming back.

"I just can't understand it," Grandma said. "As hot as it is, and an old dog like that."

"Well," Grandpa said, "he used to take off now and then when he was a pup."

Grandma made a laughing sound, although she wasn't laughing. "Yes, when he was a *pup!* But how long has *that* been?"

Grandpa turned to me. "You say you saw him lying out there by the barn where he usually is?"

I told him I had. I said he was lying there in the shade, watching me.

"And you didn't go back there?"

I shook my head no.

"It is mighty strange," Grandpa said. "And that's a fact."

"He was a good old dog," Grandma said, "for all his faults."

"You're talking like he's dead," Grandpa said. "What he's done, he's just run off somewhere. He's probably back there in the woods, sniffing out some groundhog."

"Old dogs don't run off like that," she said.

Grandpa laughed. "Also, you can't teach them new tricks."

"It isn't funny, and you know it."

Grandpa turned back to me. "And you didn't see him later on when you went to hoe the sweet corn?"

"No," I said, "I guess he must have taken off by then."

"It is mighty strange for a fact," Grandpa said; and Grandma looked hard at my face, gazing at me so intently it was if she could see everything that had ever been inside my head.

Often, throughout the years, I have told this story, precisely as it is recounted above. After all, it is a true story, and we are always interested in true stories. We come to one another asking, "Can you tell me what you know? Can you tell me what has happened to you? Can you tell me what it is like, being who you were and going through what you have gone through?"

I can understand the Ancient Mariner; we all can. An untold story is an awful burden; and even after it is told, it reverts to what it was before, an untold story. So it's no wonder.

Hector is my albatross, you might say; but that is fancy—too facile, too neat, too literary for an honest truth. This is not to say it is false; it is merely, like all prescribed meanings, too limited to rest with. But I could not disavow it, even in its faintly ridiculous coloration; I could not disavow it even if I wanted to, for it would be wrong to state that Hector does not have a special place in my memory. How could it be otherwise?

Upon those occasions when I tell the story (usually after a few drinks, let me admit), there are certain inevitable questions. I have learned to anticipate these questions, so I will ask them in a general way, along with the answers I have found best for them, as follows:

QUESTION: Did your grandparents ever find out that you had killed their dog?

ANSWER: I don't think so. But since that time I have learned something about the secret bureaucracy built into human perceptions, so I would have to admit that I am less certain now than I was, say, twenty years ago.

Q: Did they continue to be as loving as they had been before?

A: I think so.

Q: Why were you living with your grandparents? Were your parents dead?

A: I lived with them only that summer. My mother was dying of cancer in the city. My older sisters stayed at home and helped Dad. But it was more convenient, and I'm sure, more humane, to have me out of the way.

Q: Why didn't you mention this about your mother in the story?

A: I don't know.

Q: Do the others in your family know this story?

A: No. My parents are dead. And my sisters know nothing about it, so far as I can tell. I'm sure that years ago they heard that Hector had disappeared, but the information couldn't have meant much to them. They hadn't gotten to know the dog as I had. And, after all, a dog is a dog.

Q: Did your mother die that summer while you were away?

A: She died on September 4, at six A.M., two days after my grandparents had brought me back home so that I could start school. She died in the hospital. They let me visit her twice before she died.

Q: Did she know you?

A: I think so, in a general way. But I can't be sure. She was deeply sedated, of course; and . . . well, you know, *dying*.

Q: What did your grandparents think had happened to their dog?

A: They seemed to think that Hector had simply run off, and perhaps had been killed on one of the back roads. Or maybe shot or poisoned. There were some sheep farms in the area, and understandably, sheep farmers use every opportunity to kill a stray dog. Or a runaway.

Q: Did they ever suspect you?

A: I think that is possible, although I can't be sure. Maybe there was a faint suspicion.

Q: Is it possible that Hector's body was ever dug up by other stray dogs and discovered by your Grandfather? Or perhaps discovered in some other way?

A: That possibility has often occurred to me, but I think I covered the spot pretty well. I did a lot of hoeing in the corn during the next few days. But of course, I have no way of really knowing.

Q: By that answer, I assume that you do not believe your grandfather would have confronted you with such evidence if something like that had happened.

A: No, I don't believe he would have. I couldn't conceive of his doing that.

Q: Is this because you think his love for you was too great?

A: Partly. But there would have been pride, as well.

Q: What does pride have to do with it?

A: I was his grandson.

Q: I see. If they had suspected you, exactly what would they have suspected you *of?*

A: I think they would have suspected me of having done exactly what I did in fact do.

Q: That's if somehow the dog's body had been uncovered.

A: Yes. Although, I think I buried it deep enough. Still, you can never know about something like that.

Q: Of course. But what if the dog's body had not been uncovered. Might they still have suspected something?

A: Yes, I think that is possible.

Q: But wouldn't that have been a rather bizarre hypothesis for loving grandparents to make about their grandson?

A: Perhaps. But they had been children once. Just as we all have been.

Q: Do you still hate dogs?

A: I have never hated dogs. In fact, I think of myself as a dog lover. Certainly, I like most breeds of dogs better than I like cats . . . which doesn't mean I'm a cat *hater*, necessarily; I just think of cats as belonging instinctually to girls and women. I realize this is a stereotype. But stereotypes are always true; their problem is, they're never true *enough*.

Q: Why, exactly did you kill Hector?

A: Well, for one thing, I was afraid of him. One day earlier that summer I saw him attack the milkman I've mentioned; and it was a shocking thing to witness. I wish I could think of a more shocking word than "shocking"; but that word comes near to it—that is to say, I felt an almost physical *shock* when I saw Hector start that damned trotting with his tail wagging, headed straight toward the milkman—who was just minding his business on the loading dock—and leap at him. Fortunately, the milkman saw him coming, and swung a heavy milk can at him, and then kicked and yelled at him . . . all of which helped. You see, there was something wrong with the dog. Maybe it was in his genes; maybe it was old age—but even then, there had to be a genetic component, because not all old dogs turn vicious. I am aware that referring to behavior as "genetic" often verges upon the mystical; but then, I am something of a mystic . . . which someone once said is the "religion of blockheads"; but never mind that . . . we don't know how accurate that person's thinking was, even if the definition does have a bit of style.

Q: Didn't your grandparents call the dog off when he attacked the milkman?

A: Oh, yes. Grandpa saw it, and went running at Hector, yelling at him with every step, and finally chased him back to his territory around the barn.

Q: Why didn't you mention this when you told the story?

A: I don't know.

Q: So, when your grandfather chased Hector away . . .

A: If he hadn't, he would have surely gotten to the milkman eventually, and there's no telling what would have happened.

Q: Yes, I see. So you killed the dog because it was vicious.

A: That was part of it, certainly.

Q: What was the other part?

A: Well . . . in a way, I wanted to see if I could do it.

Q: By doing it, you mean, kill the dog. Kill a living animal. Creature.

A: Yes.

Q: So it was something of an experiment.

A: Yes. How else does a child learn?

Q: And you were testing your skill and . . . *courage*, perhaps by killing your grandparents' pet dog.

A: It wasn't as simple and cruel as that makes it sound. Saying it that way.

Q: I assume that your mother was too sick to know about what happened.

A: Of course. Not only that, nobody *knew*.

Q: I mean, about Hector's "disappearance."

A: How would a dying woman find energy to think of something like that?

Q: Was your mother's death a great loss to you?

A: Certainly it was! What do you take me for?

Q: So there were two deaths that summer which have stayed with you all these years.

A: It's grotesque to have you pair them like that, but I see what you're getting at. And, I suppose the answer would have to be, yes. But that's a little like coupling a tornado and a spring rain under some such rubric as "Meteorological Observations."

Q: Perhaps. Do you ever dream of Hector?

A: Yes. Now and then.

Q: What sorts of dreams are they?

A: I can't actually remember very much. Usually, I wake up remembering that I have been dreaming about Hector, but I don't remember much of what has really been happening in the dream.

Q: You dream of your mother, too?

A: Of course. And I see where you're headed, and . . .

Q: Certainly. I understand.

A: We are all initiated into death by various routes, but in a way, they're all alike, aren't they?

Q: Perhaps. But about Hector . . . is it that you just see his image in the dream?

A: Yes, sometimes. I guess you could say that. Sometimes I just see him lying out there in the shade of the barn, watching me. The way it was that day. Almost as if waiting for me.

Q: Do you ever dream of him getting up and starting to trot toward you, wagging his tail?

A: Yes. Sometimes I see him do that. And then I wake up.

THE FARTHEST REACH
OF CANDY NIGHTS

Dept. of English
Prairee State University
Morristown, Ill. 60113
Feb. 18, 1985

Pamela Schurz
Dept. of Creative Writing
Iowa College
Whitman, Iowa 53106

Dear Ms. Schurz:

I have been following your most successful career as a novelist and
short story writer for the past decade, and rejoice in the renown you
have achieved. Not only that, I have read every book that has "fallen
from the press," as they used to say, and have found all of your work
rich with subtlety and inventiveness.

Is it possible that you remember me? I "taught" you creative
writing in our beginning workshop here at Prairee State. You were
in my 119 class, "Introduction to Fiction Techniques." You may re-
member me as the portly old party with sideburns who used to scold
you over such matters as "logical connectiveness" and "point of
view." How long ago that seems, even to me! To you, so much
younger, it no doubt seems another life, another world.

My reason for writing you will no doubt appear very strange:

I am wondering if I could arrange to study fiction with you at Iowa College next Fall term. I will be on sabbatical then, and would welcome the opportunity to come there if you think I could be admitted to your creative writing program as a special student. The oddity of my request deserves something in the way of an explanation. Perhaps you will remember (if you ever knew, and there is no particular reason you should) that I had had a number of short stories published when you attended Prairee State. These stories appeared in such periodicals as *Muddy River Review*, *Patchwork*, the *P.S. Quarterly*, and *Initiational*. Such modest publication credits were sufficient to "qualify" me to teach beginning creative writing at Prairee State, but I am afraid they must represent pathetically little by today's standards, especially as compared to your own remarkable achievements as a nationally, indeed internationally, famous writer.

Nevertheless, they were accomplishments of a sort, and I cherished them as one cherishes "his own" (whether children or artworks). However, I have had very little success since that time, and have had to come to the realization that for some reason, in some way, I am not writing stories that inspire today's readers or, for that matter, and perhaps primarily, today's editors. Therefore, I am not at all ashamed to "face up to reality," and write to one of my erstwhile students—especially one who has accomplished so much!—and try, if I can, to "crack the code" that is necessary for publication in today's markets.

There is no feeling of humiliation in my doing this. I hope you will understand; and also, I hope you will not feel embarrassed on my behalf for coming to you "with hat in hand," so to speak. The logic seems to me irrefutable: since you have so admirably achieved "the right voice" for one who, it happens, once was judged to have the right to teach you. Times change, and so do literary proprieties; I am asking that I might avail myself of the opportunity to learn how to ride "the new wave" and discover, somehow, whence it has come and whither it is going.

Aware that the preceding sentence sounds alarmingly old-fashioned, I will leave it, simply adding that it is precisely one of the things I must "unlearn":—a chore that my close reading of your books convinces me you, more than most, could teach me.

Please forgive this long-winded letter. May I add that succinctness is one of the qualities I most admire in your own writing? Alas!

Yours truly,

Edward J. Treece
Associate Professor
of English

Creative Writing
Iowa College
Whitman, Iowa 53106
Feb. 24, 1985

Dear Professor Treece:

Your letter struck me as curious enough, and believe me I get some curious ones. I guess you'll have to apply through the regular channels, just like everybody else, even for admission as a special student. Although I don't see any particular reason that you couldn't come here. It's okay with me if you're in my class. I can stand it if you can.

To be truthful, I don't remember you. But then a lot has happened since those old days at Prairee State. You're right, it was another world.

Anyway, send along your academic record to the Grad. Chairman (I can't think of his name at the moment), and see what happens. It'll be nice to see you, I guess . . . since I can't actually remember you, it wouldn't be honest to make such an assertion without a guess.

Good luck.

Yours,

Pamela Schurz

P.S. One thing: I never use quotation marks except in dialogue and generally advise against it. P.S. (Again.)

Dept. of English
Prairee State University
Morristown, Ill. 60113
Feb. 28, 1985

Pamela Schurz
Dept. of Creative Writing
Iowa College
Whitman, Iowa 53106

Dear Ms. Schurz:

Thank you for your letter of Feb. 24. I am deeply pleased that my request did not seem too "quirky" to you. Oops! I should delete those quotation marks! See? I have already learned something useful: "never use quotation marks except in dialogue." (Please note that I assume that this exception extends to literal reproduction of words used by another, verbatim, as I have just done with yours from your post-script.)

Enclosed is my short story, "The Farthest Reach," which I hope you will find satisfactory and—why not?—enjoy. It is, as you will note, a story about reversal and self-doubt. These are common themes, of course, but worthy of celebration again and again, if they are done with grace, style, and insight. I hope you will find my story worthy in such ways.

Also I enclose my old academic record, along with a vita sheet. The former I dug out of leaves in my files, dusted off, and packed into the fat envelope you have just (presumably) opened.

Happy reading! And I hope to renew our acquaintance next fall, in a classroom not unlike that in Swearinger Hall, where we first met all those years ago. Situation reversed, of course.

Yours truly,

Edward J. Treece
Associate Professor
of English

Creative Writing
Iowa College
Whitman, Iowa 53106
Feb. 24, 1985

Dear Prof. Treece:

Your packet of materials arrived safely, and I have forwarded everything but your letter to the Graduate Chairman, whose name I've finally remembered: it's Adelaide Potter. (And here I was thinking it was a man. Oh well.)

Ever since your first letter arrived I've been trying to remember which one you were, but so far, no luck. I guess I can't remember anybody there, practically, except for a young grad assistant named Ron Klippinger. He had long hair, I remember, and sat on his desk. Pretty good teacher, all things considered, although I can't remember what it was he taught. Probably something at the finger painting level, though.

Anyway, good luck with your application. You should be hearing before long.

Yours,

Pamela Schurz

P.S. I generally don't read MSS. submitted for grad application unless there's something questionable about them. You know, if they straddle the line for admission or something like that. Anyway, good luck. P.S. (Again.)

Dept. of English
Prairee State University
Morristown, Ill. 60113
March 14, 1985

Pamela Schurz
Dept. of Creative Writing
Iowa College
Whitman, Iowa 53106

Dear Ms. Schurz:

Thank you again for your so-prompt response. Here's hoping your review committee will find my story, "The Farthest Reach," acceptable for your program.

It saddens me to report to you that Ron Klippinger was killed in an automobile crash two years ago. He had been a valuable member of our English Department since he received his Ph.D. here (which must have been when you were an undergraduate student) although he was somewhat "far-out" for the more conservative members of our department. (There go these pesky quotation marks again!) Still, it was a tragic loss. Perhaps you remember Professors Reed, Walshick, and Rabin, too: they have all retired. Professor Ray Gorsuch, whom I'm certain you knew, passed away untimely just before Christmas. He seemed to be in good health, so the shock was considerable. He was only 55. Professor De Long may have retired shortly before you came; he was a distinguished old man with a vandyke and hearing aid. He died last year, aged 89.

Sorry to be the bearer of so many bad tidings, but it is surely best that you know these things, for they have had to do with your own life, however peripherally.

I hope you agree. And I also hope that you will like "The Farthest Reach," should you have the time and opportunity to read it.

Yours truly,

Edward J. Treece
Associate Professor
of English

Creative Writing
Iowa College
Whitman, Iowa 53106
March 23, 1985

Dear Prof. Treece:

No, I guess I don't remember any of those people, except for Ron Klippinger. Sorry to hear he was killed. He was always something of a hotshot, as I remember. Anyway, they say it will happen to all of us, one way or another.

No word on your story, yet, but I had a few free moments and thought I'd scratch off this note to you.

It will seem odd having one of my old profs in class, but I don't mind. Why not? I've never been what you'd call a shrinking violet, so I won't be inhibited, even if I remember you. Which isn't much of a certainty, since Prairee State seems pretty much a dark spot in my career when I look back. I don't know why this is so. I don't suppose it's because you didn't have any effect on me or anything. After all, everything has an effect. Especially upon a writer.

Yours,

Pamela Schurz

Dept. of English
Prairee State University
Morristown, Ill. 60113
March 28, 1985

Pamela Schurz
Dept. of Creative Writing
Iowa College
Whitman, Iowa 53106

Dear Ms. Schurz:

Thank you again for your letter, this of March 23.

By coincidence, I have just purchased a copy of your literary magazine, *A Whitman Sampler*, and am puzzled by one of the stories in it. This is a story titled, "Oregon or Bust," by a writer named Janis Oritz. I'm afraid the story is something of a puzzle to me. Why does the narrator keep saying, "Deprive me of my periods and I'll write forever?" I assume this has a specifically feminine as well as grammatical significance, but I don't see what any of this has to do with the story of diving for treasure off Corfu. And I am perplexed by the title, although the Or of "Oregon" and the conjunction "or" repeat the first two letters of Ms. Oritz's surname.

Would you say that this story is representative of what *A Whitman Sampler* is looking for in their fiction? I ask this, seeing that your name is listed among the "Advisory Editors," and supposing that if you don't actually read manuscripts, you nevertheless find some common ground of sympathy and sensibility with the editorial policy of the magazine.

Thank you again for your interest in my application. Indeed, I do look forward to being "in your class again"—although I'm afraid that, to the world's way of looking, I am not at all in your class, and not likely to ever set foot there.

Still, one must do what one can.

I remember one class meeting when you fell asleep on the shoulder of a boy named Nick Reynolds. Do you remember that day? When I stopped talking and simply sat staring at you, you didn't seem at all fazed for a long moment and then you opened your eyes widely and stared all about you. Several of the students laughed nervously, but you didn't say a thing. You took it all very much in stride. I must say, I admired your poise, even though I was sorry to have put you to sleep.

Once again, I hope you have an opportunity to read "The Farthest Reach," which I consider the best thing I have ever done. Of course, that may not mean a great deal in terms of "today's idiom." (Creeping quotation marks again; but I don't have the heart to delete them, so I'll let them stand.)

Truly Yours,

Edward J. Treece
Associate Professor
of English

Creative Writing
Iowa College
Whitman, Iowa 53106
April 18, 1985

Dear Prof. Treece:

I nearly always fell asleep in class when I was at Prairee State. It was a chronic condition with me. That's probably why I don't remember much of what went on there. Mind elsewhere, on more interesting things. Even while asleep. Nothing personal, of course.

I still haven't read your story. As I think I explained, I usually don't have a hand in making the decisions, except in borderline cases. So you may hear from the Grad Chairman, Adelaide What's-Her-Name, before you hear from me. Or *instead* of hearing from me. Choose one. Or neither.

Concerning your comments on Oritz's story: no comment.

Yours,

Pamela Schurz

Dept. of English
Prairee State University
Morristown, Ill. 60113
April 26, 1985

Pamela Schurz
Dept. of Creative Writing
Iowa College
Whitman, Iowa 53106

Dear Ms. Schurz:

No doubt you're getting tired of hearing from me, but I am taking the time to write to you to admit that my judgment of Ms. Oritz's story might have been somewhat premature. It seems to me that the "randomness" built into the narrative line is nothing to alarm a sympathetic reader. Certainly, modern literature has come to terms with such randomness . . . perhaps, even, has institutionalized it.

At any rate, I want you to know that Ms. Oritz's story is not so chaotic for me as it was at first reading. Certainly she has demonstrated a flair for metaphor. Something of a "metaflair," perhaps.

Hoping that this letter finds you thriving and productive, as I know must be the case.

Truly yours,

Ed

Creative Writing
Iowa College
Whitman, Iowa 53106
April 18, 1985

Ed:

Your story found its way to me this morning, accompanied by such comments as: "I thought this went out with the likes of Trollope" and "Where did this guy come from? He writes like he's two hundred years old!"

These first readers did not have any way of knowing that you were not the typical grad school applicant, of course; so their judgments have to be considered honest. At any rate, I read the story and I'm sorry to report that what you're doing here doesn't seem to be anything that people have taken seriously for decades, if not the century or two these readers suggested.

I'm sure somebody, somewhere, might like this sort of story, but to me it just seems like so much bullshit. I don't like to sound harsh, but you deserve to know the truth, and I'm candid enough to give it to you.

So there you are. It seems as of the moment that there's no place for you in the program here. No doubt you'll be happier elsewhere. You'd probably find us a big pain in the ass, and we wouldn't be too comfortable with you, either.

Yours,

Pamela Schurz
Encl.: MS of "The Farthest Reach"

Dept. of English
Prairee State University
Morristown, Ill. 60113
May 22, 1985

Dear Ms. Schurz:

Your letter of May 16 received. I would like to say that I was more shocked than surprised, if that makes any sense. Perhaps it is true even if it doesn't.

Naturally, authorial vanity whispers to me that you haven't actually read my story, even though you no doubt think you have done so, and could not understand how I should say you have not. But then, most authors feel this way about their work, and it is pathetic that such should be the case.

At any rate, I want to thank you for whatever sympathy you've extended to me over the past few months, during our exchange of letters. Probably it isn't sympathy I need at all, though; in which case, I hardly know what to pray for. Certainly, to the very limits of what critical insight I've been able to cultivate over what I hope is not a totally misspent career, I must cry out to you that my story, "The Farthest Reach," whatever its faults, is vastly beyond the realization of anyone who could take Ms. Oritz's story seriously, for Ms. Oritz's "story" is nothing more than a mindless narcissistic exercise in self-indulgence.

But I will not expect you to be in tune with such a judgment, nor will I expect you even necessarily to understand. I remember one day in class when you refused to listen to a boy's story that had to do with his being initiated into pheasant hunting by his father. As I remember you stalked out of the class—to the dismay of some, and the more-or-less secret admiration of the remainder.

But no matter. There is no particular reason that our two worlds should meet. Evidently, from all that you've said in your letters, they did not meet then, in that direction; and now it appears that they have not met (and obviously will not) here, in this other.

I have just read your recently published volume of short stories, *Candy Nights,* and since candor is of the moment, I feel that it is only just to inform you that in all honesty I have to say that your work is not as interesting as I had at one time thought. Just "for your information," as the memo pad says.

Yours truly,

Edward J. Treece

P.S. I can't help pointing out that in your letter of March 23 you refer to having "a few free moments." A "moment" is not a specific temporal unit, therefore one cannot reasonably speak of having a "few" of them.

Creative Writing
Iowa College
Whitman, Iowa 53106
June 1, 1985

Professor Treece:

I remember you now. I'm glad you're not coming here.

Pamela Schurz

BEGOTTEN SPIRITS

Blood is a hot, sweet, temperate, red humour, prepared in the *meseraick* veins, and made of the most temperate parts of the *chylus* in the liver, whose office is to nourish the whole body, to give it strength and colour, being dispersed by the veins through every part of it. And from it *spirits* are first begotten in the heart, which afterwards by the *arteries* are communicated to the other parts.

Burton, *The Anatomy of Melancholy*

Late Tuesday morning. Greg's mother phoned him at his office and asked him to stop by for a short visit Thursday afternoon. He was a little surprised that she'd called him at work, and he wondered if she was all right, since it had been under three weeks since his father had unexpectedly collapsed and died while reading on the sofa in their game room.

"Don't you usually get off early on Thursdays?" she asked.

"Sometimes when I have a golf date," he answered.

"Well, could you manage to stop by this Thursday?"

"Sure. I guess so. What's it all about, anyway?"

"It's just something I'd like to discuss with you. I'm sure Sherri and the kids won't object. They can spare you for half an hour, and so can your golfing companions."

"No doubt. And as for Sherri, I think she'd prefer my stopping off to visit my mother to playing my weekly game of golf at the Club."

"*Weekly* game! Don't try to sell that story to me. You play on

Saturdays and Sundays, too, if I'm not badly mistaken. And if Sherri isn't misled as well."

Greg laughed dutifully. "All right, I'll stop by. But I'm naturally curious about what it is that you can't talk about over the phone. And even if I do play golf this Sunday, why don't you come over for dinner again, and we'll talk about whatever it is?"

For a brief moment his mother was silent. Then she said, "No, Greg, this should be just the two of us. It's something about your dad. Indirectly, anyway. It's nothing really earthshaking. But Sherri and the kids would be bored."

"Now I really am curious. You know Sherri's not bored by family matters of any sort. And the kids can always amuse themselves. What in the hell are you up to?"

"Please don't speak to me that way."

"I can't believe I'm hearing this. Since when have you gotten so stuffy?"

"What you call stuffy . . . is well, maybe it has to do with your father's death. You seem to forget it's only been a little over two weeks."

"No, I haven't forgotten. Not even three weeks yet. Okay. I'll see you Thursday."

"It shouldn't take very long, Greg."

"No problem. I'll stop by. I won't even mention it to Sherri."

"Now, don't be that way. Of course, you should *mention* it to her. It's not anything that has to be kept secret. Just don't make such a big thing out of it. You practically pass my house on your way home, so what could be more natural than stopping in to see your mother once in a blue moon?"

"Okay, no problem. And you're right, I'd planned to get off early for golf, but that can wait. About two or two-thirty okay?"

"That will be perfect."

"Just one thing: it's not about the will, is it?"

"No, it's not about the will. There's no problem with the will. Absolutely not."

"Well then, I really don't see why you can't talk about it over the phone."

"You'll understand Thursday."

Greg looked down into the mouthpiece and said, "Sure. Okay. See you then."

Rita, the maid, answered the door, which was always kept locked, and told him his mother was in back, by the pool. A ten-foot, white-painted brick wall surrounded the property, so there was no entry except through the front door or the garage, which was always closed, or one of two black metal gates in the wall that could only be opened by punching out a six-figure electronic code, which rang a soft alarm and canceled if the wrong number was punched. The release code was intricate and responsive, but the systems had been installed after his marriage, so Greg had never bothered to learn it.

He said hello to Rita, asked how she was, and then threw his light silk jacket over the stained cherry banister of the central hall stairway as he passed it and walked down the dark hall, toward the lighter area of the game room in back. He walked through, glancing at the large, comfortable leather sofa where his father had been sitting and reading a book when he'd suddenly collapsed and died eighteen days before, and then ambled out the sliding screen doors to the patio. The brilliant sunlight struck him almost palpably, shards of brilliance reflected from ripples in the pool, along with the wrought-iron lawn furniture packed with fat green and yellow pillows, placed here and there on the flagstones of the patio as well as upon the lawn.

His mother was sitting eighty feet away, under a beach umbrella near the pool. On the table beside her were a tall, empty frosted gin and tonic glass and a thick leatherbound book. The bulky morning paper lay on a flagstone beside her chair.

"Why don't you buzz Rita and have her fix you a gin and tonic," his mother said, after they'd greeted each other.

He nodded. "Sure. Do you want one?"

"Yes, I'll join you."

He nodded at the empty glass on the table. "It looks like it's the other way around. I see you've already had one."

"All right, if we're acting boorish today. Be it noted, however, that I've had only one."

He buzzed Rita, ordered two gin and tonics, and sat down. "So noted, but I thought you and Dad made it practically a moral issue never to have a drink until five."

"Greg," she said, closing her eyes and leaning her head back against her chair, "for God's sake, don't be difficult. Now of all times."

He gazed at her a moment. She had kept her figure remarkably well; she was still a very attractive woman. What vitamins, plastic surgery, and the pampered life, he was thinking, can't do for a woman!

This notion struck him as neither pleasant nor decent, and he frowned briefly as if publicly embarrassed.

Eyes open, she'd noticed. "What's wrong? Bad day?"

Greg sighed. "No. No big deal. Just hard, not really bad. We get them now and then."

"Don't I know!" she said, nodding. "Don't I remember from the days before your father retired! Relax, I won't be keeping you long."

"Now, don't start talking like that. I'm perfectly comfortable and I'll enjoy a leisurely conversation. And a drink. Good God, what do you take me for?"

"Here's Rita now."

Rita placed the two gin and tonics on the table and departed.

"Mud in your eye," Greg said, lifting his glass.

"Mud," his mother responded, lifting hers.

The ghost of his father's voice, repeating *Mud*, echoed in his mind. He frowned and sipped. "So there's no problem with the will. Right?"

"Right. The will is just fine. 'Tight as a drum,' as Barry states the matter."

"Good old Barry."

"Don't know what we'd do without him."

"But you've got something else to discuss."

His mother's gaze unfocused as she stared out over the lawn. Then, with her voice slightly more distant, she said, "Tell me something, Greg; and I want you to answer truthfully. Right now—right at this very minute—do you smell anything?"

"Do I *smell* anything? Of course not. Why, should I smell anything?"

His mother shook her head. "Nothing? No unpleasant odor of any kind?"

He shrugged, then sniffed. "Well, the flowers and grass. But they're certainly not unpleasant. And the lime in the gin and tonic. What else should I smell?"

"Nothing. I merely asked."

Gazing at his gin and tonic, Greg nodded. "So are you coming for dinner Sunday?"

"Let me think about it, all right?"

"Of course. But you know how . . . I mean, these first few weeks, especially. You know."

"Of course I know."

"What have you heard from Babs and Rick?"

"They call every night. Babs wants me to come stay with them for a while. Rick and Ginny are getting ready to go to Europe. The kids are all in school. Everything's fine. I let them know that you and

Sherri are taking good care of me. And Kitty and Thelma and Rex are all keeping in touch. You know, your father and I had wonderful, wonderful friends."

"You still do."

"I know. I didn't mean it that way, exactly."

"What's the book?"

His mother turned her head slowly and gazed at it lying there on the shaded surface of the table. "Yes, the book. Well, I guess I shouldn't beat around the bush any longer. The book is why I asked you to stop by and talk with me this afternoon."

"Oh?"

She nodded. "Do you know what it is?"

"Damned if I do. I can't see the spine from here."

"It's the book your father was reading when he died."

"Oh."

"It was his favorite book, of late. Silly expression: *of late*. And not exactly accurate in this case, because he liked to read from it off and on for almost as long as I knew him. Anyway, he'd been reading from it over the past few months. It was almost like he just couldn't seem to get enough of it."

Greg sipped his gin and tonic. "So, what is it?"

"It's a book he bought right after he went into practice, forty-five years ago. It's a valuable book, you know. When he bought it, we thought it was really extravagant."

"Sure, but I assume it has a title. So, what is it?"

"It's Burton's *Anatomy of Melancholy*. It was first published back in the 1600s sometime. Not this edition, although this is a very valuable one, published by some private press in England. I can't ever remember the name. Anyway, your dad had it specially bound by that man in Italy years ago. I can't remember his name, either. Honestly, my memory! But it was our second trip to Europe, and he brought the book with us."

Greg nodded. "Sure, I remember. He was always talking about it."

"*Quoting* from it. You've heard him quote from it practically all your life. Surely, you remember."

"I guess so. Only he didn't always cite the source of a particular quotation, you know. He was always laying one quotation or another on us."

She glanced at him sharply, and then put her hand out and turned the tall frosted gin and tonic glass around in a circle without lifting it from the table.

"You say he was actually reading it when he died."

"Yes."

"I knew he'd been sitting on the sofa, of course. And I guess you told me he'd been reading. Naturally, what else? I mean, he read every evening, practically. But I remember it was just the two of you together in the game room."

"God, it was *so sudden*, Greg! Like something out of nowhere. He just keeled over." His mother's voice almost broke. "I know I've told you all about it, and I hate to go on and on, but. . . . Well, I'm only glad he didn't suffer. That's all I can manage to be thankful for at this stage, I guess. I know I've told you about it a dozen times, but it still seems so unreal. I keep thinking if I put it into words often enough, it'll turn into something I can believe and, you know, *handle*. You always hear about things like this, but when they actually happen to *you*, you somehow can't. . . . I know that's a platitude, but the truth of the matter is . . . "

"Sure," Greg said. "Just take it easy. What the hell, it'll get better."

"Sure," she said. "What the hell."

For a moment they were silent. Greg looked up as a slight breeze fluttered the leaves of the poplars lining the south end of the pool.

He took another sip and said, "Did you have your swim this morning?"

She shook her head. "I just can't bear to do it alone, Greg. Not yet. Dad and I had done it too long together. I know it sounds silly, but that's the way it is."

"Sure. It'll come in time, I guess."

"I guess."

Greg frowned at his glass. "What's this you were asking about some smell? Some odor."

When she didn't answer right away, he looked up and saw her nod at the book. "You know, your father hemorrhaged terribly. It was so awful, so sudden! Blood just poured out of his nose and mouth, and the instant I looked, I knew he was going. His eyes were so terrible. It was unmistakable. They were glazed. And the expression on his face was . . . oh, in a way, it was a look I'd seen a thousand times. Sort of patient, and even understanding. Even in that brief instant, he knew. But I knew that look, and it was like this was just another thing he'd had to go through. I'm not sure that makes sense."

"Sure it does. And I know it must have been awful."

"When you say things like that, it makes it sound as if he weren't . . . hadn't been your father!"

113

Greg twisted uncomfortably in his chair. "For God's sake, give me a break, will you? Do you think I don't feel it too? I know it's got to be harder on you than anybody, but for Christ's sake, Mom, I . . . "

She laughed and then began sobbing. "You haven't called me 'Mom' for so long I can't remember the last time."

"What are you talking about? What do you think I call you? What else *would* I call you, for Christ's sake?"

"You don't call me anything. Just, 'Hey, you' or something."

"That's not fair, goddamnit, and you know it."

"No, I don't suppose it is. And I'm sorry I've somehow managed to ruin your visit already."

"Forget it. Only, I had an idea there was something specific you wanted to talk over. That's why you wanted me to stop by—something that you couldn't talk about over the phone. Remember? But if you don't feel like it now, well, that's okay, too. Whenever you're ready. Okay?"

"I suppose I should apologize for acting that way."

"Forget the apologies. If you feel like talking about it, whatever it is, all right. If not, it can wait. No sweat."

She nodded. "No, it's about the book. It's . . . well, the thing is, Greg, that book has his *blood* all over it. About ten or twenty pages just ruined. I don't know how many. I haven't exactly counted them, you know. But when it happened, the blood just gushed out, and . . . " She stopped and shuddered, with her eyes closed.

"Look, take it easy, will you? I know it had to be an awful thing to see happen, right there before your eyes, but . . . "

She shook her head. "That's not the way to look at it. I'm only glad I could be with him right up until the very, very last minute."

Greg nodded and took another drink. "Well sure, I guess I can see it that way, too."

"I have phoned several bookbinders, and they all say the same thing."

"Which is?"

"Those pages are absolutely ruined. And so is the book."

"I think I'm beginning to see."

"You do see, don't you?"

Greg nodded. "Obviously, it should be thrown away, only . . . "

"Oh, God, how could *I* ever throw it away? It was the last thing he was reading, and it had brought him so much *pleasure*! Not just these past few months during his retirement, but when he'd first bought it, even. And when he lugged it to Europe with him, and read from it in the evenings. And had that Italian bookbinder bind it in fine pigskin. Do you know he paid eighty dollars for that binding? And that was back in the days when some men paid sixty dollars for a *suit*."

Greg finished his gin and tonic. "Well, I don't know what to tell you. I mean, I can see how you'd naturally feel sentimental about it and everything, but . . . "

"Greg, it *stinks*! I'm sorry to put it that way, but it's true: it *stinks*! When blood rots it turns absolutely putrid. *Anybody's* blood, of course. Somehow it doesn't seem fair, does it?"

"No, I don't suppose so." He thought a moment. "What if you put it out in the sun, like today? The smell would eventually go away."

She nodded somberly. "Eventually, I suppose it would. But then I'd have it in the house, *with his blood still in it*. I honestly don't know how that would make me feel. For some reason, it seems just too ghastly to contemplate."

"I wish there were something I could do."

For a moment his mother was silent, gazing at the water in the swimming pool. Deep in thought, she stroked the glass that held her gin and tonic. Finally, she said, "As a matter of fact, I believe you can, if you'd be willing. And I honestly, truly hate to ask you. But the thing is, I've got to do something, and yet I just can't bear to throw it out. Do you understand?"

"Sure."

"You do see, then? I know it's silly, but you do understand, don't you?"

He nodded. "Of course. But you don't really have much of a choice, do you? I mean, what are your options? Blood is blood, and it is also animal matter, and when animal matter rots, well, no matter whose blood it was . . . to put it bluntly, it turns to shit."

"Greg, please don't talk like that."

He shook his head, and suddenly realized he was perspiring. "Jesus, it really was a bitch at the office today. Maybe I'll have another one." He got up and buzzed Rita.

"Greg, please don't use language like that. When you were in your teens, you had to show off and use it, but you should be well past that age now."

"Sure. I'm well past it."

"I don't think I should have another one. Two's enough for an old lady in my condition."

"You're not an old lady and you're in great condition and you know it."

"Well, it's sweet of you to say so. But sometimes I wonder why it's worth it any more . . . or why it *will* be worth it, from now on. It was always for him, you know."

"Sure, I know."

"And when you think of it that way, you must realize how impossible it is for me."

"Why don't I just take the book with me and toss it. Okay?"

A terrible silence fell upon them.

Rita appeared with Greg's gin and tonic, placed it on the table, and left.

After a moment, his mother said, "Could you? I mean, it wouldn't be the same, would it, if you did it?"

"Of course not. It wouldn't be the same at all."

"And it's not like any part of him remained somewhere, *watching*, or any superstitious nonsense like that. And yet, I've been thinking about it: for me it would seem like a betrayal. But it wouldn't really be like that for you, would it?"

"Of course not."

"Maybe if you'd been living at home . . . or if you'd been with him the evening it happened, it would be different, somehow. But now, it's just . . . well, I guess the way to look at it is, it's just something that has to be done."

"No problem. It's only a thing, after all. A physical object. No more than, say, an old sweater or a pair of shoes."

But she wasn't really listening. "You see, it's more than the smell; because, you're right, I could put it in the garden shed or someplace, and I suppose that eventually the smell would go away."

"I understand perfectly. It's the idea of having those pages stained brown with his blood. His *life* blood, as they say."

She reached over and touched his arm. "It really is different, you know. I don't think there's anything wrong with you doing it; but if I did it, it just wouldn't be right. If he hadn't loved the book so damned much . . . "

"I know. We agree on that."

"And there's no reason you can't tell Sherri. I mean, it's not like it should be a big secret, or anything. Because what's disgraceful about it? And Sherri is as sympathetic and understanding as a woman could ask for. I mean, to have as a daughter-in-law."

"Of course not." He sipped at his gin and tonic thoughtfully.

"Although, I didn't want to discuss it in front of her this afternoon. You understand that part, don't you?"

"Absolutely. So let's just forget it. Consider it over and done with. Mission accomplished, practically. Decided upon, anyway. *Agreed* upon."

For a moment they sat without speaking. Greg took another sip of his gin and tonic.

"The weather *is* lovely. Maybe you can still get in some golf this afternoon."

He inhaled abruptly and said, "Well, I think maybe I will take off and try to get in a few holes. I've still got to work on my approaches. How I ever got the slice out of my drive and not out of my long approaches, I'll never understand. I've practically given up on the goddamn three club."

"I know you'd like to be out on the golf course. And I can understand it. Your dad played golf when you were little. Then he gave it up by the time you were, oh, I guess fourteen or fifteen. Along about then. You know, I'm not really sure whether he just lost interest or got too busy. How close we were, and yet how much I don't know! Even though that's a little thing, still it was part of him."

Greg carefully placed his half-empty gin and tonic on the table. "Well, he may not have known himself. Everybody makes decisions without being aware of all the reasons. But, now that you mention the weather and golf, maybe I will be toddling along. You'll let us know about Sunday, won't you?"

"Of course."

He stood up, put his hands on his waist, and stretched his back. "Needless to say, we hope you can make it."

"I know I'd enjoy it. I'll call Sherri tomorrow, if that's all right."

"Sure. Plenty of time."

He half turned, and his mother said, "I'm so glad you stopped by."

Greg nodded and headed back toward the house.

"I'll come with you," his mother said, and Greg said, sure, that would be fine.

"But you mustn't forget the book." She held it out to him.

He frowned and took it from her. "Of course not. Talk about absent-minded."

"Your dad was that way, too. It's in . . . good Lord, I started to say, 'it's in the blood'!"

"Genes," Greg said, and she nodded.

When they were in the hallway, he said, "You know, I suppose I could just store it somewhere in our own shed at home, away from everybody so the stink wouldn't be a bother. And then, after the odor was gone, I could advertise for another copy—maybe an imperfect copy, only with those pages still in good condition. And I could have a bookbinder insert them. I'm sure that could be done without much trouble."

Near the front door, he stopped and regarded his mother. The expression on her face was thoughtful and distant.

He shrugged. "I mean, it's an option we hadn't considered, isn't it?"

"I guess so. I hadn't thought of it."

"And I noticed that there doesn't seem to be any blood on the leather."

"No, it's all on the paper. And it was all over his shirt and slacks, of course, which I've thrown away. He just sort of instinctively set the book aside when it happened. Very slowly and deliberately, as if he didn't want to drop it or something."

"Of course, it might not be all that easy to find another copy. Some of his books were very rare. Was this one of them?"

She frowned. "Well, as I said, I'm sure it was valuable, and everything, or he wouldn't have spent eighty dollars to have it rebound by that Italian binder. But I suppose you could find another copy somewhere, if you tried hard enough and were willing to bide your time."

"Then maybe we should think of something like that."

For a moment she gazed above his head, blinking slowly. Then she lowered her gaze and smiled tiredly at him and patted his hand. "No, I don't think that would be smart. For one thing, it would be too much trouble. Really. And you shouldn't be silly about such things. It seems to me I've been silly enough for both of us already."

He shook his head. "I don't really see it like that."

She patted his hand again. "Well, you're just being kind, and I appreciate it. But we might as well go ahead with our original plan."

"Okay. It's up to you. So I'll toss it."

"Yes," she said. "Toss it. And give my love to Sherri and the little ones. And while you're at it, just go ahead and tell them I'll be there Sunday. Tell them I'm looking forward to it."

"Sure," Greg said. "I'll tell them. They'll be glad to hear it."

His mother held her cheek up for Greg to kiss, and then he carried the book out to his BMW and put it on the front seat beside him while he turned the ignition key and started the car. When he drove away, he looked in the rear-vision mirror and saw his mother still standing in the doorway, waving good-by to him as if he were departing on a long journey.

Twenty minutes later, he arrived at the Coffee Hills Country

Club, where he threw the book into a large, hooded, green-metal trashbin that stood by the side entrance. It seemed to him the ideal place for such a deposit, because he had to admit that he shared a little of his mother's superstitious uneasiness, and the idea of taking the book home and throwing it away there was subtly disquieting. Odd as it was to admit to himself, he felt that it was far better not to take it home, even if the garbage truck came tomorrow. Something in him didn't even want it to lie there in the trash overnight, in their garage, as if it were a contaminating presence, and it was better to keep it at a safe distance until it was burned or buried or suffered whatever fate lay in wait for the trash picked up at the Coffee Hills Country Club.

THE RIVER

It is broad and swift, and
flows in darkness, winding its tortuous way among wooded hills and
rocky cliffs that loom against the dull light of the sky at its brightest.
When the night is clear, these massive protuberances of Earth cast
their shadows onto the surface of the water, obliterating great irreg-
ular expanses of moonlight and starlight.

The riverboat churns heavily upstream against the strong cur-
rent. Its portholes and windows are all alight, giving the stubbornly
laboring vessel a bright and festive appearance as it plows through
the water. But in spite of all these lights, no one can be seen on deck.
No one can be seen through the portholes, walking, or dining, or play-
ing cards. No one's face is visible in the portholes, peering thought-
fully at the river waves as they pound, plash, and occasionally surge
against the deep-plowing hull.

This river does not flow in daylight. Always, wherever it flows,
it is night. Therefore, all the lights of the riverboat are kept on as
it makes its way upriver. Sometimes, heavy rains fall splashing upon
the deck, making the light from the portholes glisten upon the wet
painted wood of the capstans, gunwhales, and lifeboat. Occasionally
snow falls; and there are even times when ice grinds in massive jagged
herds upon the broad expanse of the river, gnashing and crunching
under the prow of the riverboat as it labors powerfully forward toward
its distant and murky destination somewhere upstream.

Most pleasant, perhaps, are the spring and autumn breezes that
flow out of the dark hills bordering the river. Even though they are

land breezes, they bear the heaviness of a distant and forlorn dampness, as if remembering those deep, mystical waters that are the source of life. They also carry delicate traces of odors that savor of time itself, smelling of oak, hickory, sumac, poplar, and ash. During the silent night of summer, the splash of an occasional fish or turtle is audible over the deep-throated chug of the engines. Perhaps, it can be imagined, the journey is not as lonely as it must, nevertheless, always seem.

Now and then, in every season, the lights of other riverboats cast their shimmering fulgence upon the rippling silken sheen of the river's surface. These other boats are of various sizes, traveling at different speeds; and, while some are lighted in every window and porthole, others show fewer lights, as if the others had burned out and there were no bulbs to replace them. Occasionally, a pathetic boat will be observed with only one or two of its lights dimly visible through what must be dirty panes of glass. One wonders what the pilot house of such a boat is like, and what that boat's ostensible destination must be.

It is not known that riverboats ever travel with any of their lights deliberately turned off. Given the nature of the river, it is not known why any of their lights should be turned off . . . although, to be sure, our general human ignorance in such a matter is never to be equated with truth.

Moonlight, starlight, or perhaps the lights of the riverboats themselves occasionally reveal the jagged superstructure of craft that have sunk. A spar or smokestack can be seen jutting from the water, upon occasion, necessitating a deviation in the course up the channel. Now and then, the flickering image of a smashed hull can be observed on the glistening mudbars, or cast diagonally upward on the banks. Now and then, more astonishingly, something oddly like a pale, blind human face rises out of the dim current, its soft, shy glow flickering once or twice before disappearing. Now and then an arm seems to lift sleepily from the darkness of the water, as if beckoning numbly for help.

Never, however, does the riverboat pause, for these human images are hardly to be thought of as real; and it is assumed that all who are connected in any way with the riverboats know about them. The likeliest technology available for such calculations is channeled into the pilot house, where charts are consulted regularly and an occasional pull upon the bell rope sends forth a great, shivering blast from the steam whistle, as if announcing the craft's continuing triumphant progress upward into the spiraling depths and channels ahead.

Steadily, the riverboat churns forward. For a very long time, there is neither pause nor hesitation in the revolutions of the mighty turbines. There is the smell of iron, oil, coal, and, now and then, perhaps, the tobacco of a thoughtful engineer as he smokes his pipe and gazes into the various physiognomies of the gauges that face him in obedient attentiveness.

In spite of its great breadth, the river grows narrower the farther one travels upstream. Such is the nature of rivers, we are told . . . and so believe. Occasionally, a great dark hole can be seen in the bank to the left or right, signifying the mouth of a tributary. One would reasonably expect the river to be narrower immediately upstream from the tributaries; but the truth is, such strictures are not always evident— even though it must be assumed that, eventually, the narrowing is there. Such narrowness is simply not as measurable and immediate as one might think if the river were simpler.

But the knowledge of such things is always present. A great yawning blackness upon the bank signifies what may be considered another opportunity; and it is known that riverboats often take these channels into other realms, forsaking the main channel of the great river, itself. But how could this be known for certain? Who is to say, when faced with a tributary of enormous width, that it itself is not the main channel, while the supposed channel is the tributary?

There are awful stories of those riverboats that choose the wrong channels and find themselves in darker, shallower streams, destined to founder or run aground. There are rumors of riverboats that have turned up tributaries that soon become mere shallow runs, with great vines entangling the mast and fouling the wheels. It is said that sometimes their dead hulks can be seen in the moonlight, festooned with creepers and vines, and ashen pale from the seasonal scrub of wind and rain.

Often, on quiet nights, the distant sound of dying horns can be heard, forlorn and desperate, like the mooing of cows that have wandered mindlessly into quicksand and cry out in dumb terror and dismay.

And yet, gradually, inevitably, the channel does narrow, no matter how skillful the navigation—no matter how shrewd the choices among tempting vistas of moonlight or starlight upon great beckoning stretches of water. The riverboats continue upstream, largely thoughtless of their destiny; yet all filled with desperate strength, as if never fully unconscious of the terrible odds against arrival.

Because their fate is certain, as is the fate of all things. Eventually, a single light in a window or porthole of the riverboat—certain of the correctness of every single choice among the tributaries—will burn out. Then, within days or months, another will be extinguished.

Thus it is that the riverboat changes, becoming like those others that have been seen far off to the side, laboring less swiftly toward their destination.

It is known that, eventually, after long dwindling, it will find itself entangled in the thick growth of vines from great trees that overarch the river. The river itself will have gotten so small it will seem that a mistake must have been made. Surely, this is not the great broad river once embarked upon! Surely, another choice would have kept one churning upstream under the stars and moon, forever hopeful and alive, with all lights merrily lit, casting their bright glow upon the waves!

But none of these lights can be replaced or relighted once they are extinguished. The smells of oil and ozone drift swiftly away upon the wind from the high dark cliffs and hills that line the river. Another light on the riverboat is darkened; then, still another. The bow lights and stern lights tend to last longest; but of course they, too, are mortal. Deep in what we call the bowels of the ship, the engineers labor in darkness, fancying that they can read gauges when the darkness is so smudged and dense even the deep, pounding sounds of the turbines are altered.

But these changes are not as sudden as the telling of them suggests. There is almost time to adjust to them; there is almost time to learn to think of them as natural after the lights have gone out. But then, it is soon obvious that the water itself is not the same. Certainly, it is not as swift; it is more sullen and dense than the water downstream. Such an impression has often been noted, and has been recorded in innumerable logs.

There can be no avoiding the fact; the riverboat is laboring in an intensified darkness. No doubt it is now indistinguishable from those pathetic craft so often noticed downstream, pushing their way slowly into the darkness, with only a dim sparkle of light here and there. And yet, it must be understood that the pilot house is always dark, for it is out of darkness that light is best seen . . . and perhaps it is now, after these various failures of illumination, that the relative brightness of the journey's beginning can be sensed and fully understood.

The riverboat is surely different. Darkness within and darkness without. There is a cold, thready, insistent rain rattling upon the wood, the metal, the panes of glass. The engines cough, and the wake might prove to be the color of phlegm, if the darkness were not so profound. The channel is uncertain, a muddled path losing itself like the estuarial fan of the muddy delta far astern, at the river's mouth.

For by now the mudbars have thickened, and the rivulets are sulky and shallow. The engines groan and spit mud; the drive shaft lurches against the sucking pressure of a medium too dense to travel through. There is a crash of birds out of the dark trees, almost overhead—startled by the sudden roar of the engines in their death agony.

The bell rope is pulled, and the great blast of the horn goes out, reverberating over cliffs and hills that now loom unseen beyond the trees that choke and clutch at the straggle of water. The noise of the riverboat's horn booms like a cannon, and the ponderous, swift stroke of the engine increases, whipping cords of vegetation all about as the riverboat leans to the side and slowly strangles deep in the midst of life.

The terrible blasts of the horn begin to fail. The noise diminishes, squeaks and pants ridiculously, and finally moans softly into silence. The hot metal ticks no louder than the chittering of a squirrel as it cools, and the last light is extinguished. Has it perhaps driven up a tributary, abandoning the main channel? Will its superstructure now glint briefly like ice, as seen from the riverboats still churning their way upstream?

Now, it can never be known that the riverboat chose wisely. Everything has come to an end. In the silence that follows, there is only that other sound. It is distant and varied, similar to the mooing of cows that have wandered into a mire and know that they can never escape, for they, too, have reached the end of all that they can understand.

Perhaps there is comfort in the notion that others have foundered before this. The skeletons of their hulks have been visible far downstream, almost from the start. The riverboat has reached farther upstream than many have, and there is something like satisfaction in this realization.

Yes, such a notion is good, beyond question, if you love the river; and if you have not dwelt too long upon the dream of a world filled with sunlight.

POISONOUS FLUIDS

This was a time long ago when only the recent model cars had shatterproof glass; but if a student had a car, it was likely to be an older model. And if one of them got drunk and smashed a car up, the glass would fly like shrapnel, causing God knows what spectacularly bloody damage to human flesh.

Our fraternity was always one of the top three on campus. I keep reminding myself of how important that seemed back then. It was, and that's that. But even though we were one of the top fraternities, most of us didn't have cars of any sort, with or without shatterproof glass. Most of us didn't need a car, for our campus in those days was small, and most necessities were conveniently near. You have to understand that this was long ago—a time when drugstores served malt-ed milkshakes and students wore thick sweaters and saddle shoes and said things like "gosh" and "gee whiz." We really did live in another world. But then, what world isn't? This was still during the Great Depression. You have to remember that part, too.

All things considered, I guess we were pretty lucky. Virtually all of the brothers served in World War II, and three that I know of were killed, two in action, and the third, Phil Twitchell, in a jeep that turned over in the Philippines. He was probably drunk. Most of us keep in touch. Also, most of us naturally became officers, for ROTC was required of all male students, and whoever graduated was in line for a commission. It didn't require much of us; but I've found that few things in this world do. You understand this about most things after they're over.

But the story I have to tell has nothing to do with those brothers killed during the war. It has to do with what happened in our fraternity during my four years of college. Several things, and then one thing especially. For example, I remember late one night after the spring prom when Bill Heckinger and Betty Todd were killed. He ran off the road in his old 1934 Plymouth and rolled down a steep bank. I got there right after it happened.

I was a junior then, and I'll never forget coming upon the highway patrol cruiser, and two other cars that had pulled over, with their headlights still on. I had a date with a girl named Mary Jo-something. Ollie Seborg and his date were in the back seat, and I remember how Ollie breathed out the word, "Jesus!" when we saw that it was a car that had gone off the road. We didn't know who it was at that time, and we stopped on the berm with our engine running, looking, and watched a man wildly waving a flashlight back and forth as he huffed up the steep bank from the wreckage, and with his throat sounding tight, Ollie said, "Oh, my God, it's Bill Heckinger's car!"

This was about two in the morning, and Ollie and I had drunk our share of beer, but I can remember how stone sober I suddenly felt when we sat there with the lights flashing over us, suddenly realizing that it really was Bill Heckinger and Betty Todd. It's funny how I can remember her name, but forget the last name of my own date that night. Mary Jo-something. But she was a girl I didn't date very much; and this was before I met the girl who would become my wife.

I heard one of the patrolmen say an ambulance had been called, and should be there in a few minutes. The other patrolman said, "Well, it doesn't matter now. There's no reason for them to hurry."

Our dates stayed in the car while Ollie and I climbed down the bank to take a look, and then, before he got back in the car, Ollie threw up in the weeds alongside the road. I remember how the pedeet frogs were so loud in the cool, fresh night air, and how clearly I could hear them between the sounds of Ollie gagging and coughing and spitting out swaying, silvery strings of vomit in the bright moonlight. There were ponds at the edge of the field, and the stars were out, and a bright full moon.

Everything was very sharp and clear, and one of the patrolmen had held his flashlight for us to see as we looked inside Bill's smashed car and saw his dead body lying there with his face all bloody and smashed out-of-shape, and the dead body of his girl cramped half-underneath him, with the steering wheel column bent crazily to the side, and glass and blood everywhere. This was the first time I'd noticed that the features of someone who's been killed by violence look smeared, somehow, as if they have been half rubbed out by a pencil eraser. When we told our dates what we'd seen, they both started wailing, and Ollie kept hiccuping and saying, "Jesus!" over and over.

Later on, back in the house, I vomited, too, but I think it was from the beer, as well as remembering how they'd looked. It was as if I hadn't felt the full impact right away, but it had to be processed, somehow, and it took time for me to realize this was the corpse of Bill Heckinger. One of the brothers, for God's sake! I wondered why Betty hadn't been thrown through the windshield; but, as they say, you can never tell what will happen in an accident. She was a small, pretty girl with dark hair and a mole on her cheek. I remember she'd had a good alto voice and had sung in the Junior Glee Club.

One of the brothers had died before this. It happened when I was a freshman pledge, and a senior named Fred Lubell died of pneumonia one night. This may seem hard to comprehend today, all these years later. It's hard to think of a healthy young twenty-one-year-old boy dying of pneumonia, but it happened. They didn't even have sulfa drugs yet, let alone penicillin. It was during a flu epidemic, and half of us had come down with it, only it hit Fred harder than most, and the flu turned to pneumonia. He was a strong, heavy boy, and the doctor came to our house that cold, snowy, dark night, only a week after New Year's, and left some pills.

Later, they said the doctor thought Fred might have survived if he hadn't been overweight. This was a somewhat peculiar idea back then, in the Great Depression, when most people, even if they were educated, still believed that generally the huskier or fatter you were, the better. But everybody agreed that doctors could have some peculiar ideas. One of the brothers, Jim Wicker, was in pre-med, and he said he'd never heard of how you could be too husky for your own good. But that was then.

There was only one other death in our house during my four years there, but this is the one I want to tell about. It happened just after Homecoming, in the fall of my senior year. Since that time, I've often thought of how the three brothers who died when I was living there in the house each died in a different season. This obviously doesn't mean anything, but I think about it anyway, because such symmetry strikes me as somewhat odd. Not earthshaking, of course; just odd. But maybe that's sufficient reason for mentioning it. The boy who died was a first-quarter sophomore, and he was the little brother of one of my three roommates, Larry Pilchard. (We slept four to a room on bunk beds in the House, which was huge, even before they built the annex in 1958.) The term "little brother" seems inappropriate, because the boy who died was a big, blond farm boy. His name was Paul Wurtz.

I know that we had a reputation as a party frat, but I don't think we were necessarily the worst. Still, the drinking this night I am talking about was heavier than most. I don't remember the occasion, but none was really needed, of course. If it was a weekend, near a weekend, or anybody's dog's birthday, it was an excuse to party. This must have been a weekday, because most of us didn't have dates; but we'd gotten a keg of beer and were taking it apart in the big basement game room. The game room was paneled in dark pine and had an oak floor. There were two pool tables in it, along with a real bar that had been donated by T. K. Secrest, an alumnus, brother, and wealthy industrialist, three years before.

We were all pretty drunk, and for some reason Larry got it in his head to start pestering Paul Wurtz. Maybe what he did was caused by more than the beer; maybe it was partly caused by a basic underlying boredom. I've often thought that boredom has more of a role in alcoholism than people think. Along with fear and frustration, of course; although everybody seems to understand those factors. However, all of them have to do with what used to be called "character"; but nobody seems to talk about character any more. I think that's too bad. And it certainly doesn't mean that character's not still a factor; it just means that people don't talk about it. Or see it for what it is. No more than that. A lack of maps never means the territory isn't there.

But whatever the reason, we were drunk, and Larry kept razzing Paul Wurtz, telling him to chug-a-lug his beer like a man and a brother. In retrospect, I seemed to remember thinking that Larry was coming on pretty hard; but it wasn't the sort of thing that anybody noticed too much at the time. It was only later, when you could draw a circle around it, that you realized what had been happening. Pledges were often pretty crudely treated, and there was always the Old-Fashioned Razz, when they had to take insults and do outrageous things; but Paul was past that stage now. He was one of us, and didn't have to do whatever the older brothers said. Still, there had always been a sort of numb docility about him, and Larry had always been pretty much of a hard-nose. So when he got on him that evening, Paul just sort of reacted obediently and without question, doing his best to keep up with the rest of us.

One thing that Larry kept harping on that night was how Paul had been a nondrinker when he'd joined us. So he goaded Paul into chug-a-lugging "more than his share and a trifle to spare," as the saying went. And Paul was drunk enough that he went along with him. He was staggering and mumbling by the time we went to bed, but we had seen that often enough. Not only that, we were doing a little staggering and mumbling ourselves. I can remember some of those dreary early mornings when the sounds of one or more of the brothers vomiting was enough to send you back to the Methodists.

But of course, what we couldn't have possibly foreseen—or, at least, this was the way we thought of it later—was that Paul Wurtz was so woefully goddamn drunk that night that he would get sick and throw up in his sleep and choke to death in his own vomit. This was in his room on the third floor. (When it came to room assignments, we worked our way downward in the old house, sophomores and pledges on the third and fourth floors—practically an attic—and brothers with senior standing in the preferred lower rooms.)

I can remember how we were awakened the next morning by the sound of Dick Singleton crying out, "Oh, my God! Oh, my God!" I don't believe that the old-fashioned Methodists, with all their eloquent gifts for repentance, could have exceeded the agony in Dick Singleton's voice. I also seem to remember a cold rain falling that morning, although this could be something I imagined later, adding it to the horror of being so godforsakenly hung over and waking up to what we had to wake up to. Don't tell me the memory isn't theatrical.

Naturally, Larry Pilchard took the news hard. Our housemother, Mathilda Simpkins, fixed hot tea for him and tried to soothe his nerves by talking to him. Mathilda was old, fat, and comfortable, and wore her hair in an old-fashioned way, with dark, wet-looking curls over her forehead. She also wore dark eyeshadow, which some of our parents thought verged upon harlotry, but Mathilda was fat enough and homely enough that nobody really complained. I always thought she looked a little like Marie Dressler, and said so one time, but everybody laughed and said that dated me. Everybody was very conscious of being up-to-date, and for the most part Marie Dressler was identified with the silent films of the 1920s. Anyway, the brothers seemed to like Mathilda well enough, although she got a bit wacky now and then, and often suffered from what she called "sick headaches," which rendered her utterly helpless.

On this morning, however, nothing she did helped, and Larry climbed back upstairs and threw himself onto his bed, facedown with his pillow over the back of his head. I went downstairs, and later, he joined us in the lounge in back, just off the kitchen and dining rooms, where we were playing poker. He walked past us on his way to the refrigerator, padding on stocking feet. He was a mess—his shirttail was out, his eyes were red, and his hair was mussed. He didn't look at any of us or speak.

"Old Larry's in bad shape," Bill Murphy said, folding his hand facedown on the card table and leaning back in his chair to look out into the kitchen.

A moment later, Larry came back in carrying a beer and shaking his head. "Jesus!" he said.

There was no answer to that, except for Brad Woolson slapping a card onto the card table.

"Do you know something?" Larry said to no one in particular. "I killed him. As sure as hell. I couldn't have killed him any quicker if I'd held a gun to his head and pulled the trigger."

"Come off it," Bill Murphy said. "The poor son of a bitch choked to death on his own puke. You're hung over, that's all."

But Larry didn't accept that. He shook his head and muttered, "What am I going to say to his parents?"

"What do you mean, his parents?" Dick Schultz said. "His father's dead. He was raised by his grandparents and his mother. *You* know that. They've been here. Good farm folks. Hell, you introduced me to them"

Larry nodded. "I know. Which makes it all the worse. So, what am I going to say to them?"

"Come off it," Bill Murphy said. "Everybody was drunk. It was just one of those things."

"Listen, he was my little *brother*, for Christ's sake!"

I didn't say anything, but when Larry said this, I thought of that corny old line in the McGuffey Readers. A boy is carrying this little kid, and somebody asks him if the kid isn't getting heavy and he isn't getting tired of carrying him and the boy answers, "No, he's not heavy, he's my brother."

Under better circumstances, I might have quoted this to Larry, trying to kid him out of it. I might have quoted that line, and everybody would have had a good laugh, and Larry would have joined in, eventually. But obviously this was impossible now, so I kept my mouth shut.

Bill Murphy said, "What I want to know is, where did you get the beer?"

Larry looked at the bottle in his hand, as if he didn't know how it had gotten there, either. "Oh," he said after a moment, "there are ways."

"If Mathilda sees you," Bill Murphy said, "it'll be your ass."

Larry shook his head. "I couldn't care less about something like that."

Brad Woolson said, "Don't worry about it. Mathilda just went to her room. I think she's coming down with one of her headaches."

But Larry didn't seem to be listening. "I really did, you know."

"Did what?" Bill Murphy asked stupidly. I could have told him, but Murphy was not what you'd call sensitive to such things.

"Killed the poor son of a bitch," Larry muttered. "My own big little goddamn brother."

"Listen," I said, "we're all just as guilty."

Larry looked at me out of his bloody eyes and slowly, deliberately shook his head back and forth, two times each way. Then he took a drink from his bottle of beer, swallowed, and said, "Oh, no, we're not."

The funeral was to be held in the Baptist Church, at the request of Paul Wurtz's mother. I was asked to be a pallbearer, along with Larry Ganz, Bob Churney, Bill Murphy, Dick Schultz, and, of course, Larry. Arrangements were made through Mathilda and Stan Bricker, our chapter president. It was Stan who got the phone call and announced the pallbearers the next evening at dinner. Mathilda was absent, still living in retirement with her headache.

"I can't do it," Larry muttered. In a way, he was as drunk as I'd ever seen him, only he was lucid drunk—if that makes any sense. There seemed to be an awful look of awareness in his eyes. Or maybe it was just alertness. But it was something you noticed.

"Sure you can," Bill Murphy told him.

Larry just shook his head dolefully, then stared down at his plate without eating.

"I don't know about the rest of you," I said, "but I'm going to eat my dinner."

This didn't make a whole lot of sense, and I'm not sure why I said it. But the instant the words were out of my mouth, Larry looked at me out of bleary eyes and almost nodded. I think it was at that instant that I realized how much I disliked him. There was something dreary and nasty about him that seemed to have been latent for the two or three years I'd known him, but was now manifest. And the oddest part of it all was that Larry himself seemed to realize this. Along about then I began to think maybe he was right, after all; maybe in every important way, he really was guilty of murdering his little brother, Paul Wurtz, just as he'd been trying to tell us.

Immediately after dinner he went up to Stan's table to talk, and I remained seated at our table, watching. I studied him as he gesticulated angrily and whispered. I had forgotten how thick his lower lip was in profile, and how his chin receded. He made me think of a story I'd heard about some poor Englishman in a Guards regiment who wasn't promoted because the hair on his head didn't grow quite right.

Stan frowned out at nothing and listened to him, then shook his head no. Larry still argued, but Stan wouldn't budge. It was perfect pantomime, and the message was unmistakable. Larry wanted to get out of being a pallbearer, but Stan reminded him that it would be unthinkable that Paul's big brother wouldn't act in such a capacity. It would be the last thing he'd ever have to do for him, Stan would say. I could almost hear him saying it.

Larry finally gave up and walked away, erect and bleary-eyed. I don't think he knew that I'd remained sitting there at our table, watching the two of them; but Stan did, and as Larry left, he looked at me and raised his eyebrows as if to say, "Well, what in the hell are *you* looking at?"

In answer, I raised my eyebrows, too, as if to say, "So what?"

But none of this really made any difference, because Larry showed up at the funeral and behaved himself, more or less. Of course, he was totally drunk, and probably didn't even remember attending the funeral at all. I'm sure this part had nothing to do with boredom; it was guilt and fear, and since then I've come to believe that it was guilt and fear of an intensity seldom found in the common mixtures of our lives.

Paul's mother was a short, wide, homely woman with an incongruously long face. His grandmother was withered and wrinkled, and his grandfather a tall, skinny old farmer with big, useless hands and a bald head. He seemed permanently tilted to the side. All three of them were so dazed, I don't think they would have reacted if someone had introduced Larry to them as the boy who'd killed Paul.

As for Larry, he sat to my left, next to the aisle, looking drunk, numb, and dismal. The preacher obviously had no idea of who Paul had been, or who his family was, but managed nevertheless to sound properly dolorous and remind us of the obvious things, reading the ever available Twenty-third Psalm.

I watched Larry as he pointed his face at the minister and tried to appear to be listening. For the few seconds that I watched him, I seemed to see everything there was to see in my fraternity brother: his utter, naked meanness, his cowardice, his immaturity, his forlorn, self-pitying regret, which made all his other vices glow with the heat of egotism, precisely opposite to how a healthier kind of regret might have cleansed and renewed his spirit.

Furthermore, it was the only time I can ever remember seeing either man or boy swallow with his mouth actually hanging open. I wouldn't have thought it possible, but somehow Larry managed. I know it happened, because I saw his Adam's apple bob, and he didn't close his mouth. This is a small detail; but our lives are made of such things, after all.

Larry's expression was so perfectly adenoidal in its stupidity that it was only with great effort that I managed to turn my head back to look at the minister, who was uttering consolation into what had to be faces eloquent with expressions of astronomical bewilderment. But I'm sure this wasn't the first time he'd had to perform his dreary function under such circumstances.

A quartet of brothers sang our frat song, and for some reason, I got the hiccups listening to them, and damned near ruptured myself trying to keep from laughing.

Devoutly, from that moment on, I wished to be finished with Larry Pilchard. I don't think I have ever hated anyone as I hated him. I was aware of the irony in the fact that I would not have felt such wrath toward him if he had not acted so guilty—had not submitted to guilt so cunningly and had not himself turned devious and poisoned, twisting with serpentine pain from the thought of what he knew he must have done. I know this must sound fancy, but under enough pressure we tend to find ourselves turning into figures of melodrama or farce.

I do not pretend there is anything like justice in what I felt then. It is only what I remember. If I could, I would have my memories be fair as well as true. But who can alter such things? The world is far more imperfect than our words can ever suggest, and the growing realization of this can turn the gift of life sour in our mouths.

As for Larry, he stayed drunk, and no one touched him. When he staggered into the game room, we would look away—pretending to be reading, or studying, or listening to the radio, or playing cards. Occasionally, I would peek at him as he ambled past, which made me realize how little he would have noticed if we had noticed him.

The thought of this was of some comfort, and it helped me to curb my own drinking a little. Much as it shames me to admit it, I made a few jokes about Larry. My only excuse is that I was almost as drunk as he was, and there were moments when his terror seemed to seep into my mind, like an actual poisonous fluid that was leaking out of the vessel of his guilt.

No one appeared to think too much of what I said, although they laughed a little, and joined in, somewhat, with an acknowledgment of how grotesque Larry's behavior had become. In response to one of my comments, Bill Murphy said that Larry had managed to have it both ways, because he had attended the funeral and served as a pallbearer, and at the same time he hadn't done either. "I think he's living in another world," he said.

This struck me as uncommonly insightful of Murphy. I thought about his words, then nodded and said, "Yes, he's living on the planet Pluto."

"I thought he was a character in Mickey Mouse," Brad Woolson said.

I told him to shut up, but he turned to the others and said, "Hell, I thought that was kind of funny."

"Not in a hog's ass, it wasn't," I told him.

It was late the next night that Larry awakened me by shaking my shoulder, and said he had to talk to me.

"Why does it have to be now?" I asked, sitting up and running my hand through my hair.

"Because now's the only time there is."

When he said this, a nasty though interesting, notion came to me: was he talking about *killing* himself? I thought briefly that if he did commit suicide, it would be good for him to wait until summer, when no one was around. Then we would have exactly one death per season.

"Listen," he said, "I really do have to talk with you."

I shook my head and inhaled. "All right. Let me get my bathrobe on."

He waited silently while I put it on and then put my feet into my slippers.

We went downstairs in the silent darkness, and back to the

lounge, where the ticking of the grandfather clock sounded uncommonly loud. There was a metal plate on the clock stating that it had been donated by Sam Boucher, Class of 1896. Although the clock ticked along faithfully, it never had the right time, so I asked Larry what time it was, and he said, Two-forty-five.

I nodded. "Okay. How about Mathilda? Is she up or around anywhere?"

Larry shook his head and turned on the bridge lamp by the card table. "No. She's in her room with her headache. Nobody else. Just you and me."

"Wonderful," I said.

"In case you haven't noticed," he said slowly and carefully, "I'm pretty sober. Relatively speaking, of course."

"Of course."

"How are you doing?"

"Relatively," I said.

He thought about that and nodded. Then he cleared his throat. "Do you want to know something? You may be the only friend I've got left."

"What?"

He nodded. "Christ, everybody around here treats me like poison. They don't even look up when I walk into the room. But I've noticed you do. You're the only one."

I frowned and rubbed my bare ankle. "It's cold down here."

"Honest to God," he whispered, "you don't know what it's been like!"

I shook my head. "No, I don't suppose I do."

"Do you have any idea of what it's been like?"

I shook my head again. "I just *said* I didn't."

"That's not exactly what I meant, but never mind."

"Look, Larry, if the truth be known, I'm pretty goddamn sleepy."

"Yes, but you're still a brother, don't forget."

"Okay. I won't."

"Do you know something? I used to think that was so goddamn corny, about us being brothers and everything; but I'll tell you something, I don't anymore.

"No, it doesn't have to be corny, I suppose."

"You'd better believe it. But what I wanted to do was, well, talk to you for a while. If the rest of them were awake, we couldn't really talk, could we?"

"No, I don't suppose so. How come you're dressed?"

"I'm thinking about leaving."

I opened my eyes wide. "Really?"

"*Thinking* about it, anyway. But right now, what I want to do is tell you what it's been like, because if I can't tell somebody, I swear I don't know what I'll do."

"Well, why not? Go ahead."

He looked down at his hands clasped in front of him. "I don't exactly know how to come out and say it. What I mean is, it's like I've gotten *old* all of a sudden, just within the past week. I was lying in bed thinking about how *true* this is, and so I decided to come and wake you up to see what you thought about it."

"You were lying in bed with your clothes on?"

"Sure. What else is new?"

"Nothing. Go ahead."

"Well, what it is, is . . . listen, there are things I've come to understand in the past two weeks that I didn't think I'd ever understand. Things I didn't even think were important, or never even thought about at *all*, only now I can't seem to get them out of my head. Does that make sense?"

I looked at him. "Maybe."

He nodded. "Do you remember that old joke about the drunk who'd misplaced his wallet, so he got drunk again, so he'd remember where he'd misplaced it?"

"Sure, I remember it."

"Well, it's kind of like that. You're all probably wondering why I've been drinking like there'll be no tomorrow. Am I right?"

I nodded. "I suppose so. A little bit, anyway."

"I've had this impression that I was the only one who's been drinking, but I know that can't be the case. I mean, people don't stop something like that just overnight, do they?"

"They say they don't."

"Right. Anyway, what I've got to tell you is, it works."

"What works?"

"Remember the drunk? I haven't been able to think of anything else, except Paul. You know, how much I was responsible and everything. My God, I've been stumbling around here and thinking about how it was that night. Sometimes I would think so hard I couldn't figure out whether it had really happened at all or whether it was just about to happen. Let me tell you something: I've never had nightmares like that!"

"No, I don't suppose so."

"But that's not the point. The point is, I really think maybe you've been right all along. I think maybe I wasn't as responsible as I've been thinking."

"What do you mean, *I've* been right?"

"Exactly. What you've been telling me ever since we woke up that morning when Paul didn't. The first thing you said to me was that *it wasn't me alone.* I wasn't the only one who'd been riding him so hard that he drank too much and barfed and choked to death on his own vomit."

"Right," I said, closing my eyes. "Sure."

"I'll tell you something: you don't know what a relief that's been. I mean, not just knowing it, sort of; but *realizing* it!"

I nodded. "So that's why you're more or less sober. Relatively speaking."

For the first time in a week I saw him smile. "You're damned right that's why. As you say, relatively."

"What do you mean," I said between clenched teeth, "as *I* say?"

"Because that's what you just said. Hey, are you all right?"

I took a deep breath. "Why wouldn't I be? I'm fine."

"God, you don't know how good it is to be able to talk to some-body. Especially, you know, a brother."

I wiped my hand through my hair. "Sure."

He watched me, then did the same thing, wiping his hand through his hair, after which he made a face like a man who's tasted something bad. "Only, there's more than that."

"Like what?"

"Well, the more I thought about this whole business, the more I realized there was something I had to face up to."

"Such as?"

"I had to face up to the fact that I didn't really *like* him!"

"You didn't like *Paul?*"

He nodded. "That's right. And don't say he was my little brother and all that shit, because I know it. But that doesn't make any difference. And don't try to preach to me, or anything. I know we're all brothers, and I've just told you how important that is to me now; but the fact is, you can't help it if somebody you've liked and gotten along with all right, as a friend, only . . . if eventually you get so you can hardly stand to be around him, can you?"

I frowned and shook my head.

Larry reached over and tugged at the sleeve of my robe. "Listen, it's not like it's some *girl* and you give her your *pin* or something, is it?"

"Of course not. Whoever said it was?"

"Nobody ever said it was, but for God's sake, you're supposed to have a special friendship for your little brother, aren't you? And your big brother, when you were an underclassman?"

I nodded.

"Listen, can't you see how that made me feel after what happened?"

"I suppose so."

"Jesus!" he whispered, looking down at the back of his fist and shaking his head.

I don't think I've ever been more wide awake, but for some reason I yawned, and Larry's expression changed a little. He said he was sorry he'd kept me up, but he hoped I understood. I told him of course I did. Then he told me how much it had meant to him to be able to get these things off his chest. I said I understood perfectly. He repeated that statement about feeling he'd grown so much older in the past few days that there was no accounting for it in terms of time.

I told him I understood that, too.

Then we both stood up, and I said I was going to bed. I asked him if he was really going to leave. He said, "Not right now. I'm going to have to sleep on it. Or at least, I'm going to have to toss and turn on it. But I'll tell you something, I really do feel relieved. I feel like I've somehow gotten through the worst part of this whole godawful nasty business."

"I hope you're right," I mumbled.

He said goodnight, but didn't show any sign of following me, so I paused at the entrance to the hallway and asked him if he wasn't going back to bed.

He shook his head. "No, not yet, anyway. I guess I'll stay up a while and think about things. You know."

"Sure."

"Goodnight."

"Goodnight."

"And thanks."

"Sure."

"Do you know something?"

"No. What?"

"Actually, now that I look at it from both sides, I can see now that I never really *did* like the poor son of a bitch. Isn't that wild? I can see it clearly now. I probably wouldn't have ever admitted it to myself, if this thing hadn't happened."

I didn't know what to say to that, so I just turned and went into the hallway, and then climbed the stairs.

His confiding in me that night did not revive our friendship. In fact, it made us somewhat distant and formal with each other. I know why I felt this way, but naturally I can't speak for Larry. Nevertheless, I would guess that somehow he knew that I resented something about him and didn't really trust him. Maybe he even understood how much of my resentment had to do with his singling me out to confide in.

But shortly after that I met the girl I eventually married, and I'll tell you, I was so crazy about her I didn't think of much else. I certainly didn't think that much about Larry for the remainder of our senior year. And it was odd that, in a way, our being roommates seemed to separate us even farther. It was as if our being together so much required half-conscious strategies for never facing each other and talking. This, along with that strange conversation in the lounge, early in the morning when the house had been so dark and silent.

I did wonder how Larry could fail to make a connection between his disliking Paul Wurtz and his obvious part in getting him to drink too much that night. You would think such a realization would only intensify his guilt; but, somehow, it didn't work that way at all. It just didn't seem to occur to him; it was as if all he needed was to tell me the truth, as he saw it, and from that moment on he was liberated.

But he wasn't really liberated, as I'll explain shortly. A few years after we graduated, the war came and I went into the army. I served in Europe, where I was eventually promoted to captain and became the chief administrative officer for a regiment in the Medical Corps. I was never in much danger; but I did serve briefly with a burial unit— a nasty and dreary business with more corpses than anyone should ever want to see. Sometimes looking at one of them made me think of Paul Wurtz, whose corpse was the second I had ever seen in my life. And sometimes I would think of how he had been cheated out of practically all his adult life by a stupid improvised ritual at a stupid fraternity drinking party.

I lost track of Larry, but in 1959, when our class had its twentieth anniversary reunion, I heard that he'd gotten divorced and was an alcoholic. When I heard this, I realized that he hadn't really escaped, after all. That was my first thought, at least; although of course it wasn't something I could ever really know. Still, it was there, and it had a sort of symmetry to it. Sometimes I think we yearn for symmetries as much as we hunger for truth. At least, it seems that much of my life has been spent in making futile connections.

Just now, reading over what I have written makes me realize that it might be interpreted as a testimonial against alcohol. But this just isn't the case. I have drunk moderately ever since my days in the frat house, and continue to have my cocktail in the evening, along with a glass or two of wine. I can't imagine any of the brothers living much differently, although I have pretty much lost touch with all of them.

Booze has ruined the lives of many people and caused untold misery, beyond any question. But I think of these as essentially human failures, for moderate drinking can be one of the pathetically few small graces that help make our lives tolerable. People who class alcohol with other drugs are wrong. They may claim to know something about chemistry or physiology, but they don't know anything about people or history.

Most of the brothers I knew are either dead or teetering on the edge of the grave. I'm right there with the latter, of course, and will admit the fact to anyone who might be interested in hearing about it.

People think the old are lonely. Maybe some of them are, but I'm not; and I doubt if others are lonely, as the young might conceive the matter. We have too many ghosts living inside our heads and don't need the company of the living, who only get in the way.

I keep thinking of how the campus was back then, and how it has changed through the years. My wife and I often talk about it. She claims she cannot remember Larry at all, but I'm sure that she must have met him at one time or another. I dated her throughout most of our senior year; and it's hard to believe they never met. I've told her this many times; but she still doesn't remember. Then the other night she surprised me by asking about that boy who got drunk and died from choking on his own vomit.

"Wasn't his name 'Larry' something?" she asked.

"No, it was Paul Wurtz who died," I told her. "Larry Pilchard was the one who killed him."

A QUESTIONNAIRE
FOR RUDOLPH GORDON

1. How many times was this questionnaire forwarded through the mail before it caught up with you?

2. List the various things that had occupied your mind during the morning before it arrived.

3. How many of your father's paintings have you now sold?

4. Do you sense that you are nearing the end of your "resources"?

5. Do you still dream of that little boat, nosing at the dock as if it were alive and waiting for you?

6. Did you sell the painting in which your father had put the boat?

7. This painting also showed a woman, leaning over and scooping up sand; who was the little boy she was facing?

8. Do you remember that heavy cloth bathing suit, with its straps and the heavy, scratchy wool against your skin?

9. What was your mother saying as your father painted the picture?

10. Why had you been crying?

11. Were you aware of his sitting back there, farther up the bank, painting as your mother talked to you?

12. The woman had been singing a song to calm you down; what was this song?

13. Was the woman truly your mother?

14. What if she lied to you; what if all your life she merely *pretended* to be your mother?

15. What if the man painting the picture with both of you in it (not to mention the little rowboat) was also a Pretender?

16. Why would they want to deceive you like that?

17. Why were you crying before your "mother" sang the little song to calm you down and amuse you?

18. Can you remember times when they talked to you lovingly, and you felt totally secure with them . . . only to see her eyes slip nervously to the side, to look at *him* . . . and only for him to look troubled, worried, as if they had both gotten beyond their depth?

19. Can you remember the woman saying, "No, we shouldn't have done it," and the man answering, "Anyway, it's too late now to change"?

20. The little beach cottage you stayed in was painted blood red; its porch and shutters were painted white; what was behind the little cottage?

21. Do you remember climbing this steep hill one day, and having the woman cry out in fear that you would fall and hurt yourself?

22. Can you remember the smell of the pine needles and the rough warmth of the stones as you climbed steadily upward, and then turned to look into the wind, at the bay?

23. She was smaller than you, down below; and the man was smaller, too, because they existed far beneath your feet; what did you say when they begged for you to come down?

24. Why did you say "never," instead of "no"?

25. Why were you not afraid?

26. What did you see in the bay?

27. What was the name of the great ship that lay like a shadow in the haze of water?

28. Are you certain you cannot remember the shapes of the letters of her name, so that *now* you can read what was then only the mystery of print?

29. Why is the name of the ship unimportant?

30. Were you surprised when you looked down and saw that he had climbed so near, without your being aware?

31. Can you remember the dark expression of anger on his face as he reached out to clasp your ankle?

32. Did he hurt you, carrying you so roughly down through the rocks and pine trees to the back of the cottage?

33. What was the song you could hear so faintly from the cabin next door?

34. Was this the first phonograph you can remember ever hearing?

35. Was this the song the woman sang to you later, after you were taken down to the shore?

36. Were you crying because of the scolding you received for climbing the steep hill in back?

37. Do you remember the old smell of salt and dead fish that drifted in the air?

38. Where were your real parents?

39. Had you been kidnapped?

40. Has this thought ever occurred to you before?

41. Do you remember the toy revolver and holster you wore?

42. Do you remember the little suitcase they let you carry?

43. Do you remember the photograph of a man and woman smiling out at you in your bedroom?

44. What was written on the photograph?

45. Did the man and woman read it to you, so that you are certain it said, "From Mom and Dad with Love"?

46. Why can't you remember the faces in the photograph?

47. Was your *real* father a painter?

48. Was this man . . . *could* this man have been your real father?

49. Could the woman have been your real mother?

50. But how can you be certain they lied to you in other matters?

51. Don't we all lie to one another?

52. Isn't the lie we tell our children one expression of love?

53. Isn't it also an expression of our fear?

54. Can there be love without fear?

55. Is it possible that this man and this woman, even though they remember the specific moment you came out of *her* body, are still not certain that you are *their* son?

56. What is a father?

57. What is a mother?

58. What is a son?

59. Why have you refused to answer these questions?

60. Why have you sold so many of your father's paintings?

61. Why do you need so much money to live?

62. Why can't you find a job?

63. When did the woman die?

64. Were you there when her eyes clouded over?

65. Were you present when your father was run down by the trolley car in the city?

66. Did you know that his legs and back were terribly mutilated in the accident, and he was dead before the ambulance arrived,

hemorrhaging brilliant red streams against the black asphalt of the street?

67. In your opinion, did he think of you as he was dying?

68. Did your mother think of you as she was dying?

69. Why do you think you cannot answer such questions?

70. Do you see yourself in the painting with the little boy, and the mother scooping sand up in her hand, and the rowboat nudging at the dock, like a small, hungry animal desiring suck?

71. What color is the sky in the painting?

72. Why is it darker than the land?

73. Why is it darker than the water?

74. Have you sold this painting yet?

75. Is it the last of your father's paintings in your possession?

76. When you do sell it, will something break loose and drift away?

77. Will the hand be seized by a spasm, and will sand spill from it?

78. Will the child cry again, staring out upon an empty scene, while the ship fades into pale gray, leaking color out of the letters of its name?

79. Who is in the red cottage now?

80. Why do you think it is empty or torn down?

81. If your father were alive, could he reach you now and carry you back to safety?

82. Could the blood on the asphalt be thought of as your father's last and most original composition?

83. Were your father and mother as lonely as children in those last moments?

84. Would you have helped them in some way *if you could have been sure?*

85. Why do you pretend you don't know *sure of what?*

86. Have you never doubted their authenticity before?

87. Aren't there other reasons than kidnapping for stealing a child?

88. Perhaps they didn't know how you came about, and felt guilty?

89. Who can say where these things all begin?

90. Don't you understand that "these things" are the cabin, the steep hill, the boat, the sand, the man, the woman, the child?

91. Were you aware that the painting was omitted in 90?

92. If you sell it, finally, will you have enough money?

93. Don't you have the pride and the skill to make your own way in life?

94. Why does that expression remind you of him?

95. If you sell it finally, will you ever sleep again?

96. Why do you think there is no one now to sing a song to you and dry your tears and pretend to be your mother?

97. When will you stop lying in your answers?

98. Do you think even *this* would turn us away, if our hands and hearts and mouths were not packed with earth?

99. Do you truly believe that some things do not abide, beyond the habit and the way of the world?

100. Truly, this is enough for now, and somehow you must rest content with this personal questionnaire.

Love always,
Mom and Dad

BOTHERING

He had phoned at ten o'clock on Sunday morning, and she said she supposed it would be all right if he stopped by. She said there could be little harm in it, and he let it go at that.

When he drove up in the driveway, she was circling a section of hose around the wire frame. *Not turning the frame so the hose would be pulled up on it,* he thought; *she hasn't even learned to do that right.*

She was wearing her peach-colored shorts and a white blouse. She was deeply, meticulously tanned, and even from this distance— before he turned off his ignition key—he could see the tiny silver necklace hanging against the dark skin of her throat where her blouse opened.

She had looked up when his car appeared, but turned back to the hose, which she was circling slowly around the frame, her gestures like slow-motion footage of an old cowboy with a lasso. Beyond her, the flower borders were lush and thickly populated with all the familiar varieties of flowers she loved. Beyond that, the Markhams' lawn stretched to the fence border in silken neatness. He could smell the wet freshness of the grass.

"Hello," he said, walking up to her with his hands in his pockets.

She glanced as high as his knees and said, "Hello." Then looked back at the hose. The nozzle was only two turns from the end. She would circle the hose two more times around the frame and it would be all neatly arranged. Done in the wrong manner, awkwardly, with her womanly stubbornness in the method, but neatly arranged, after all.

"I was surprised you called," she said. She straightened up and slapped her hands together, as if the hose had been dusty instead of wet.

"I just thought I would," he said.

She twisted her upper body around and looked back at the lawn, as if to be reassured that it was still there, familiar and comforting.

"It looks nice," he nodded at her flower border.

"I've spent enough time on it," she said. As if she didn't love working with her hands in the black dirt; as if she were making some obscure complaint to him.

He nodded at the thought and strolled over to the lawn chair at the edge of the drive.

"You might as well sit down," she said. "If you want to."

"Might as well." He tried not to sound ironic. It had been one of the things she couldn't stand in him. She had complained that his irony had become a way of life; which is an impossible life to live, of course, as anybody knows.

She didn't join him in the lawn chair next to his, but went over to the trellis by the garage and tugged at the wisteria. "I think it's dying," she murmured, "and wisteria *never* dies." He didn't know whether she had been addressing him or simply commenting aloud, the way solitary people do; so he didn't answer. Then he wondered if she would refuse to sit next to him—perhaps remain standing for the entire duration of his visit, however long that turned out to be.

"You're looking well," he told her. "I mean, good, too." That came out sounding asinine, and she shrugged without speaking, dismissively, as if he'd just complimented someone else.

"So, how's your life?"

He glanced up and saw that she was crouched by the flower border, her knees primly together. Lovely knees, as any man could see. And remarkable for a woman her age.

He swallowed and looked at his car. "Well, I'm alone now."

"Alone?"

He nodded, not knowing whether she saw him or not.

"Then I guess it can happen to any of us," she said with her back turned.

"I guess it can," he muttered, taking his glasses off and watching the world suddenly blur into a stew of colors, not one of which was recognizable as anything at all.

The "other woman's" name was Tracy Vandecker, and when he'd first met her he thought she was so beautiful she would probably glow in the dark. Grozik had introduced the two of them: he'd knocked on the door of his office that morning six years ago and said, "This is your new assistant, Ben. Some people have all the luck."

Tracy smiled vaguely, uncomfortably, and Grozik leaned his fat belly forward with his hands in his hip pockets, rumpling his coattail out behind. "You'll find Ben easy to work for," he told her, starting to rock back and forth. His gray hair was piled on his head with a plenitude that seemed almost feminine; yet his face underneath was small, dark, and craggy—the face of a man who kept bitter secrets— and his voice was a husky masculine tenor.

"Well," he said, in the manner of one who has lingered for half an hour instead of having just arrived, "I guess I'll leave you two together."

Later, Ben pondered over this scene with Grozik, brooded over it in long, tedious intervals of surmise, wondering at the sense he could never escape that Grozik had somehow, fatefully, casually, un-knowingly, thrown the two of them together. The horror of it was that such a slight cue, given without awareness by an associate like Grozik—who had four grown children and whose only known pas-sion was sailboating . . . the horror was that such a trivial event could turn his entire life in another direction.

Ben could hear Grozik saying it over and over: *I'll leave you two together.* Things might fall apart, but this priestly, unmeant utterance lasted on and on, more durable than a marriage ceremony. At least, partially. In a way.

Indeed, it appeared that Grozik had done just that, left the two of them together. And somehow, inscrutably, Ben's divorce from Car-ol, and the few years he'd lived with Tracy, all pivoted upon that one moment in his office when Grozik had introduced the new pro-grammer assigned to his unit—a slender young woman with pale hair and gray eyes that had such a look of depth and softness that you might think she must never be made to face certain things; this girl needed protecting in ways that a man could hardly imagine.

The fact is, he had never blamed Rick for siding with his mother. It was only natural. And he had never been weak enough to assume that Carol poisoned his son's mind against him during those first days of his rebirth, when he and Tracy had been happy together, almost in the way of newlyweds; even though for Ben it was a wry and wistful sort of rebirth, leaving his wife of twenty-four years cast aside—proud, silent, and dense with misery, tending her lonely garden.

And it was because of this that Ben was not surprised that Rick phoned. He had been resting, lying on the sofa, counting his pulse. Half-asleep, and then the phone rang, and Rick said hello.

"You'll never guess," Ben said into the phone. As if he had phoned his son, instead of the other way around, and couldn't wait to tell him.

"What?" A hint of wariness in Rick's voice? Possibly.

"I saw your mother two . . . no, three days ago."

Rick was silent. So he had talked with her and knew all about it.

"She looks good," Ben said in the hearty voice of a father encouraging his son through some murky ordeal of adolescence.

"Yes, she's doing well," Rick said seriously. Ben could almost see him nodding into the receiver, and thought: *There's something in him already that's older than I'll ever be.*

"I called about tomorrow," Rick said.

"No problem," Ben said. "No problem."

"Wait a minute: you haven't heard what I have to say yet!"

"I told you before that you didn't have to help out. There's nothing I can't manage."

For a moment Rick was silent; then, in a slightly altered voice he said, "Are you sure?"

"Absolutely. One hundred percent."

"You're not holding out on me, are you?"

Good God, Ben thought, *that sounds like me twenty years ago!* "No, I wouldn't do that." His voice was suddenly hoarse, so that he had to clear his throat.

"Positive?" Rick asked, decently trying to conceal his relief.

"Positive," Ben answered, nodding himself, this time. "How much is there to haul away when you clean out an office?"

He almost expected Rick to say he didn't know, since it had been so long since he'd visited his father's office, but he remained quiet. And yet seemed reluctant to say good-bye, as if he would not be guilty of this small final betrayal.

"Are you sure the doctors say it's all right?" he asked. "I mean, lifting boxes of papers and everything. It's okay?"

"Absolutely okay," Ben said. "Listen, your old man's strong as an ox. His troubles lie elsewhere. It's not his back that's weak, but his head. You know, just a few blown fuses, that's all."

This chattery nonsense would not have deceived anyone, but Rick took it for what it was—a handle to grab, a harmless pretense that would relieve him of any obligation to come tomorrow.

"Well, if you're sure . . . "

"Absolutely. Didn't I phone to tell you I could manage all right?"

"Yes, but I hate to—you know—let you down and everything."

"Listen," Ben said, an odd sort of protective urgency in his voice, "you're not letting me down!"

"Well, if it's okay, then."

"It's okay."

He heard Rick inhale suddenly—a signal that he was about to say good-by. "It sure does seem odd to think about, though."

For a moment, Ben's throat closed like a fist, but he swallowed and nodded. "Yes, it seems pretty odd, all right. But I guess the way to look at it is . . . the way to look at it is, I should be thankful I have, you know, all that medical leave accumulated."

"Sure. Well, if you're sure, then."

"I told you I'm sure." Ben cleared his throat again. "Absolutely."

"Okay."

"She really did look good," Ben said, but the phone clicked, and he realized that Rick hadn't heard him because he'd been too late in saying it, and Rick had already started to hang up.

It was possible he'd heard him start to say something and would call back to ask him what it was, if maybe there was something else.

But Rick didn't call back, and Ben told himself it was all right, because there were a lot of things Rick had to do. He probably hadn't even heard him, which was Ben's fault, because he should have spoken sooner.

Even though he'd mentioned the fact earlier. He wasn't quite certain why he'd felt the need to say it again. That sort of compliment wasn't very much, when you stacked it against all the other things. It was very little, and even if Rick had heard it, he might have thought of it as a pathetic attempt to buy back some sort of right that his father had long ago relinquished forever.

Grozik was the last one to visit him. Ben was sitting in his desk chair with his eyes closed, waiting for the light-headedness to pass and leave him solidly packed inside his head, the way you should be.

Certainly, he didn't hear Grozik, but when he opened his eyes and swung his desk chair around, he saw the other man standing in the doorway, his hands characteristically in his hip pockets, his suit coat bunched wildly behind.

"Are you okay?" Grozik said.

"Sure," Ben said. "One hundred percent."

Grozik nodded. "The expected answer. You'd think on your last day in this esteemed establishment you'd relent a little."

"What's that supposed to mean?" Ben asked.

"Let up. Relent. Admit that you can go as low as, say, ninety-eight percent."

Ben smiled a little and nodded. *Lower than that*, he was thinking, but there'd be no good reason to lay such a truth upon another.

"Are you sure you're okay?"

"I'm okay," Ben said.

Grozik frowned. "I mean, I don't want to *persist*, or anything. You know?"

"I know."

Grozik rubbed his chin with his hand and walked over to Ben's desk, where he picked up this year's calendar and glanced at it. Then he put it back. "I suppose everybody's at you with questions," he mumbled, looking at the window. "So I won't be a pain in the ass. Okay?"

Ben nodded and swung his chair around toward his desk, which looked unfamiliar already, since he'd cleared it of everything. Four boxes of his personal belongings rested on the floor. They were small boxes, but they were pretty well filled. It was not much of an accumulation for so many years, but it was enough to take with him.

"We'll get somebody from shipping to take these down in a truck," Grozik said. "Or have you already made arrangements?"

"It's taken care of," Ben said, swinging back and forth in his chair. It was the sort of nervous movement small boys make when they have too much energy to keep inside.

"God," Grozik said, shaking his heavy head of gray hair, "I didn't think *I'd* be here to see *you* leave!"

"Things happen," Ben muttered, clasping the arms of his chair. It was a good chair, he thought; he'd put a lot of miles on it.

Grozik frowned and shook his head. "I know I said I wouldn't interfere or get nosy or anything, but whatever happened to her? I can't help wondering. I mean, I never asked, because I figured some day you'd, you know, *say* something. But now, with you leaving and everything . . . "

"She's in Washington," Ben said. "Washington, Dee-goddam-see."

Grozik nodded. "I see."

Ben removed his glasses, transforming Grozik into a watery gray smear in the light. "It was a foolish thing to do, Grozik."

"I know, I know."

"But I did it, and . . . " Ben put his glasses on, and Grozik more or less appeared before him, "that is that."

Grozik nodded heavily, a realization of a man's troubles riding on his head. "Everybody makes mistakes," he muttered. "And Jesus, Ben, she really was something!"

"Yes, she was."

"Think of it this way: how many men can ever say they've put it to something as gorgeous as she was."

"Is," Ben said. "Is."

Grozik nodded and said, "Is."

"She's still alive and kicking. And last but not least, young."

"It's a fucking shame, when you think about it."

"Exactly what it is," Ben said, taking his glasses off again. "And do you know what?"

"What?"

"It was because of our age difference. I mean, we looked at the world differently."

Grozik thought a moment and then said, "To tell you the truth, I don't see how that could be."

"Well, it was," Ben said, and Grozik remained silent.

Ben put his glasses back on. "And do you know something else?"

"What?"

"My wife used to be as beautiful as Tracy was."

"No shit!" Grozik muttered, the coloration of awe in his voice. "Her name was Carol, wasn't it?"

"Yes," Ben said. "And still is."

"Sure," Grozik said. "I mean, that's what I meant."

The prognosis left no room for doubt about the scenario: his optic nerves had been irreparably damaged, and his sight would fade before the rest of his brain stuttered and dwindled into nothing. So he would die in darkness. Don't we all, he told himself, and made vague and inscrutable preparations.

For a while he watched television, but eventually gave it up as a frivolous waste of what time remained for him. Reading had long ago become too painful; this was the immediate cause for his retirement on sick leave, in fact—his death being only a further condition beyond that . . . a sort of total and final retirement.

One of the things he began to school himself in was the impossibility of his ever going back to Carol. That Sunday visit had added nothing. It had not gone well. What monstrous strangers they had become, and how odd it was of him to have expected anything else.

Rick phoned twice a month, or perhaps once, if he was busy; their daughter, Melissa, phoned once, but eventually he was able to count six months from the date of that call. She had broken down and cried that one time, and Ben told himself that was why she hadn't phoned again—it was too painful for her. He was learning a lot of things. As for their other son, Barry, he didn't call at all, and would not. Barry was living on the East Coast, but he would not have phoned if he'd lived nearby: it would have violated something he thought of as his personal integrity.

So the months phased in and out, and the world got darker. It was odd that, after the initial blurring, the deterioration was noticeable only in the slowing absorption of light. Things were just as clear, and no clearer, than they had been that day when he had last seen Carol. But increasingly there was less light in the world.

Of course he hadn't told her, and of course she knew. She knew as surely as Rick, who phoned once or twice a month, and Melissa, who had phoned once, and Barry, who would never phone at all. Carol knew, but she did not know it from Ben, and there was a sort of pride in that. Not much, but something.

Then one day she called. He seemed to feel himself lean over into her voice as if it had been a great net and he was losing his balance. But when this sensation had passed, she was still on the phone, talking to him, saying that she thought he should come over so that they could discuss things. She didn't say what they would discuss, but he knew the sound of her voice: it was her efficient tone, the way she talked to bank clerks and insurance agents. It was her tidy, neat voice, and he had once mimicked it lovingly, assuring her that he thought it was cute. Was this patronizing of him? In a way, perhaps, but she had accepted it, for it was a kind of affection, after all, and she needed affection more than she needed pride. At least, this is the way he remembered her as being.

"Why not tomorrow afternoon?" she asked.

"I think I can make it," he answered.

She paused, seeming to consider that, and Ben wondered if she thought he might have a problem getting there, somehow. But he was still able to drive, although doing so tired him out extravagantly, and simply being outside in the light—dimmed as the world had become—was enough to make him want to climb back to his bed after a half hour's exposure. It was not easy, and it would get relentlessly worse.

"Yes," he said; and she said, fine, she would see him then.

This time, it was late autumn. It had been over a year since he'd last seen her, that late summer day when she had wound the garden hose slowly, hypnotically, around its frame, putting it to bed as if it were a goofy, tender serpent child, tired of this world unto death.

She had a fire going in the living room, and looked fresh and pretty, wearing a soft lavender sweater and glass earrings that flashed in the firelight.

"Would you like a glass of sherry?" she asked when he sat down on a sofa that had been familiar to him only a decade before.

"I guess so," he said. "Thanks. I mean, why not?"

"Yes," she said severely. "Why not? That's one reason we have to talk."

"I see," he said, actually seeing nothing at all.

She went into the kitchen for the sherry, and he sat there gazing into the twilight of the room, trying to imagine for a moment that he had just gotten up from a nap on the sofa, and that all the time in between was a fading illusion.

She returned and placed his glass of sherry on the coffee table, sitting across from him. "I don't suppose you have to wonder about what it is," she said. "You must surely be aware that I couldn't help but know all about it."

He nodded and sipped at his wine. He narrowed his eyes and looked out the window. It was late enough in the year that it would be getting dark, anyway; so it was hard to know how much of that darkness was inside and how much out there in the world.

"I guess I should have been the last person to be surprised," she said meditatively, running her finger along the outside of her knee, and gazing at it as she did so.

He nodded again, encouragingly. "You mean, about my illness."

She shook her head rapidly. "No, that is not what I mean. And somehow, it's typical of you to think of that first."

There was a whirring in his head, something turning and exercising a torque upon his vision, as if there were an old-fashioned electric fan oscillating hummingly inside his forehead, against the bone.

"The fact that you wouldn't tell me," she whispered, putting her glass down and shaking her head. He thought he could see tears in her eyes, but he wasn't sure. And then she smiled faintly, distantly (this he could see very well), and he knew that she was crying. As if in confirmation, she slowly passed the back of her hand over her eyes.

"I had to hear it from Rick," she said. "If it had been up to you, I still wouldn't have known."

He shook his head and sipped at his sherry again. "No, I guess not."

"Can you imagine how that makes me feel?" she asked.

For a moment, he thought about it. "No, actually, I guess not," he said finally, his voice hoarse again. He cleared his throat. His hoarseness was almost a symptom, lately—but whether of the disease or of his being alone and not talking was hard to say.

"You've always shut me out," she whispered.

"I didn't think of it that way."

"No," she said, shaking her head rapidly. "You wouldn't."

"I guess I thought of it as . . . well, sparing you."

She laughed bitterly. "You don't know anything in the least about me, do you?"

"No, I suppose not. If you say so."

"I do say so."

"I guess I didn't want to bother you."

"Did I hear right? *Bother* me?"

"The wrong word, I guess."

"I'd *hope* so!"

"And that's why you asked me to come over?" He gazed at her out of genuine curiosity, trying to make his glasses focus better than they were capable of.

"Not only that," she said, standing up and walking to the window he had been staring out of when he wasn't trying to see her as clearly as possible.

"It's not just the fact, Ben; it's why you would do this to me. Why you would feel that you couldn't share this with me after . . . well, after the other part of your life went wrong."

He nodded and thought for a moment. Then he was about to tell her it was because of pride, when she interrupted him, saying: "Do you know what it is? You're too proud! You always have been."

"I didn't think of it exactly that way," Ben said, looking at the coffee table and trying to see if his glass was leaving rings on it.

"How *did* you think of it, then?"

"Well, I thought of it more as *having* pride. Which isn't exactly the same thing, is it? I mean, being proud is one thing, but having pride is another. I think I'd rather have it than . . . well, *be* it."

"I see what you're trying to say," she stated in a small voice. It was her understanding voice, only it was pure hypocrisy, for he'd heard it a hundred times, but it had never led to anything like a change of mind or heart.

"It's what I had in mind, anyway," he muttered, feeling that things were slipping away from him more swiftly than ever. Surely, it had gotten too dark for this time of day.

"You were trying to spare me, is that it?"

He nodded, knowing it was no use: but the truth, anyway.

She laughed bitterly again. "After all the other things," she said, "you decided to spare me. Is that it?"

"I guess it doesn't sound very convincing, does it?"

"No, Ben, it does not."

For a moment they were silent. "Well," he said finally, "you got an explanation."

Then he paused two beats, and both of them together said, almost in unison, "Such as it was."

Old routines die slowly, old word games played lovingly throughout a marriage, old cunning at being able to predict the reaction of a spouse—both of you trapped in what you both are.

But neither of them laughed, because it wasn't really funny. Nor did they return to the central issue, as she viewed it, and by the time he had finished his sherry, Ben stood up.

"It really is getting dark," he said.

"I know," she said.

He got on his coat and hat and gloves, and just before he reached for the front door knob, she said, "You shouldn't really be driving. Why don't I call Rick, and he can take you home, and I'll take your car back."

"No, I can see well enough," Ben said. "And I don't live that far. It's no problem."

"You wouldn't say so if it were."

"I'd guess that's part of having pride, too," he said, unable to resist giving one last flourish to the idea.

Carol did not contest his statement; she did not insist upon his being proud, in contrast to having pride.

As he drove back, he thought about this. She was no fool, and must understand perfectly that it is better to possess something that can be taken away from you, because ultimately it belongs to others as they deserve it, than to be imprisoned in something like *being* proud. She would have understood this perfectly, and would still think about it.

Outside, it had actually started to snow. Ben turned on his head-lights and could almost feel the cold flakes whipped through the flood of light his car pushed ahead of him. They blew out of the darkness, and seemed not to have fallen from the deeper darkness overhead, but to have materialized from the pale fringe of air that he was moving through.

A little bit like love, he was thinking: something that you never really *were*, as being in love, but something you had, which could be taken away for any number of reasons, even when you were not aware of it. Maybe he had been in love with Tracy, and that was why her leaving him had not really torn anything away from what he was, but as for the other, it had belonged to Carol, and she had known it forever, practically. Had never forgotten it, and never would.

How many men, he asked himself, almost in Grozik's voice, *could say that they had ever possessed something like this?*

WEBSTER'S FUNERAL

Strangers to each other, the two of them met over the fresh grave of a common acquaintance.

The dead man's name was Webster. He had recently been divorced, after which he had moved over five hundred miles to this city, where he was just getting settled into his new position with Becker and Loman, when he suddenly, unexpectedly, died in his sleep of a coronary.

After the man and woman introduced themselves to each other, the man said that Webster's death showed poor timing, since he had died far from his home among strangers. He pointed out that poor Webster hadn't been living his new life long enough to have accumulated friends.

At first, the woman seemed taken aback, perhaps even shocked by the insensitivity of the comment. But then she gave the strange man a quick, searching look—as if to penetrate his mind and understand the inner meaning of what he'd said—after which she decided to laugh it off. Still half smiling, she shook her head and looked upward, as if to say, "Honestly!" For one thing, she hadn't known Webster well enough to take the comment at all personally. Also, she seemed uncertain of precisely how cynical or unfeeling the intention behind the man's remark had been.

This man and woman had known Webster at different periods of his life, neither having ever heard him speak of the other. The woman had been a recent associate at Becker and Loman; whereas it appeared that the man had traveled to the funeral, over five hundred miles from the city where Webster had lived previously.

Standing just inside the grave tent and looking around at the few people in attendance, he leaned over to her and said, "I guess I must have been the only loyal friend the poor son of a bitch had back there. It's a sad commentary on something or other. Anyway, I won't be going back until tomorrow morning, so . . . well, this may not be the time and place, as they say, and I don't want to come off as an insensitive slob or something, but what the hell, how about having dinner with me this evening?"

"You're the only one I've met from his old life," she said in a musing voice. "I'm with Becker and Loman, too. Did I tell you that? Anyway, everybody sort of wondered about it. Him. You know, the story behind it and everything. About him, that is. Of course, we knew he was divorced and everything."

"And everything," the man repeated, nodding. "But you haven't answered my question. I mean, if you're tied up or something . . . "

"No, I'm divorced, too. Isn't just about everybody?"

"Practically, I guess. So dinner's on?"

"You do come on pretty fast, don't you?"

"I'm a turtle. But I'm a lonely turtle."

"That's sort of how I viewed Tim Webster."

He nodded. "Well, maybe in some ways I'm sort of like our old friend Webster, yes."

"*Your* old friend; my new one. Or acquaintance, I guess you'd say. Fellow laborer at Becker and Loman, anyway. Whatever that makes us."

"As a matter of fact, I'm going to be coming here twice a month for a while. We have a branch here, you know. And they've put me on it. I'm their hatchet man."

"It sounds like a lovely job."

"Well, it's part of what they pay me for. And if the truth were known, it's one of the reasons I was able to make it to old Webster's funeral today. Not mixing business with pleasure, certainly . . . but business with duty, I guess you'd say. If I hadn't had to come here anyway, I guess there wouldn't have been anybody here from the old days. You'd have to be a pretty close friend of somebody to travel that far, even for their funeral."

"So you're going to be getting to know our great city."

"Cities are pretty much all alike, so far as I can see. Great, small, or medium-sized."

"I don't think that's true. Maybe if you just visit them twice a month for the purpose of eventually cutting out some of the corporate fat, they all look alike; but not if you really get to know them."

"I guess maybe I've just seen too many."

"Well, most of the people who stay here awhile get to like it."

"If they don't get to like it, they probably don't stay here, do they?"

"Probably. But I think it's more than that."

"Okay, I'm willing to be convinced. Maybe you could help me get acquainted."

"Well, I suppose it's a theoretical possibility."

"Does that mean dinner this evening's okay?"

She frowned a moment, thinking as she gazed past his shoulder. Then she looked back at him, smiled, and nodded. "Well, sure, why not?"

On his third trip, they had their third dinner together, after which they returned to her apartment and became lovers.

Their relationship was a warm and happy one for several months, and then they were forced to realize it would have to end, for his corporate mission was completed. Both were saddened by the prospect, although they managed to be practical and realistic about it.

At their good-by dinner, at a restaurant named Tosca's, she asked him how many were going to be axed because of his recent efficiency study.

"Probably not more than six or seven."

"Not as bad as you thought, then," she said.

"No. It's not as badly run as they thought at the home office, but it still had to be checked out."

"Well," she said, lifting her wine glass and looking at it, "it's been nice, and to be entirely selfish, I have to say that I for one am glad it had to be checked out."

Smiling, he reached over and touched her wrist with his fingers. "So am I, which makes two, I guess."

"So let's not be gloomy, okay?"

"Right. No gloom this evening."

"I guess I've always been one of those who thinks of the glass as half full rather than half empty."

He nodded. "I know you are, and I'm the same way. I think that's part of what we have in common; it's part of what makes us so compatible."

"Made," she said with a small, wistful smile. "Past tense, I'm afraid. Things being as they are."

"Well, I suppose it does look that way."

She frowned. "You know, there's something I was thinking of last night, and it's rather strange when you think about it. As often as we've been together, we've never once really talked about Webster."

"Why should we?"

"Well, he brought us together, didn't he?"

He smiled. "That's a funny way to think of it, but I suppose he did, in a way. At least, his death brought us together. No, not even that, exactly. It was his funeral."

"Did you ever know him well? For example, did you know his wife?"

"Oh, sure. We'd had dinner together a few times. He and my ex and his ex, and so forth. I mean, back before any of us were X's, you might say. Along with other people, of course."

"It seems like just about everybody's divorced," she murmured thoughtfully. "Somehow, it seems very sad, don't you think?"

He nodded. "Yeah, it's an epidemic. But, it probably evens out; most of them get married again. Most of us. Or make some kind of parallel arrangement. You know."

"Sure. It all works out, I suppose."

"It's strange you should bring up Webster, though. I was thinking about him, too—just the other day."

"You mean, how he brought us together? Introduced us to each other, you might say?"

"As a matter of fact, I was thinking about that."

"What else about him?"

"Well, I knew him before you did, of course. So maybe we didn't see the same person. But what I was thinking was . . . well, I guess I was thinking about how Webster was the . . . how can I put it? He was just about the saddest son of a bitch I've ever known."

"Sad?"

He nodded. "Like they don't get any sadder than Webster was. Sad. Just plain, dumb, down-home *sad*. It was almost like a sickness. Maybe terminal. God knows what was eating him up. The poor, dismal bastard."

"Don't you suppose his divorce could have explained it? God knows, they can tear your guts out. I can testify that I certainly wasn't any singing lark when I had to go through mine. And that goes for my ex, too. For a while he was talking about suicide. And I have to admit that I even thought about it once or twice. If we'd had kids, maybe we would have stuck it out, somehow, but there might not have been any triumph in that, because I think after a few more years together we would have ended up *really* hating each other.''

"I know what you mean. I don't think it was quite that bad with us, but it was nasty enough, all right.''

"Well, don't you suppose *that* could have been his problem?''

He nodded. "Webster? Sure, I don't doubt but what that was part of it. But when I think back, it seems Webster was always like that. I mean, he was like that before. As if maybe it was part of what *caused* the divorce, more than a natural result. You know, like it was just too depressing to be around a poor, morose son of a bitch like that. Does this fit the Webster you knew?''

She frowned. "Maybe, now that you mention it. Although we didn't talk all that much to each other. And how much can you say during office hours that's personal?''

"Oh, you can tell.''

"Of course. That was a stupid thing to say. But to answer your question: now that you mention it, it seems to me that he did radiate a certain gloom.''

"That's the way it was. The poor, forlorn bastard just couldn't seem to help it.''

"Surely you're not saying that he could have died of unhappiness!''

"Well, not exactly. Or not directly, anyway.''

"And yet . . . I guess if you *were* saying that, I'd know what you meant. I've often thought there are more ways of killing yourself than poison or a gun.''

"Of course. It happens all the time.''

She smiled brightly. "So the moral is, stay happy and stay alive. Right?''

"If you're not happy," he said, "you're not alive to begin with.''

"My, how sententious! But I guess you could put it that way.''

"But the point is, old Webster's funeral brought us together, didn't it? And in case you're wondering, from my vantage point it's really been a lot of fun. I mean, wonderful. As I say, if you want to know.''

"Of course I want to know, but you've told me before. Still, I don't mind it when you repeat things like that. Especially when I feel the same way, and especially *tonight* when it looks like . . . well, like we're not going to be seeing each other again.''

"Hey, let's not make it sound *too* final. Who knows? Not only that, it's always best not to think too far ahead.''

"I know. Maybe they'll assign you to another hatchet job here again."

He smiled and patted her wrist again. "Sure. Maybe some time. Why not?"

"But now I guess it's sort of ending."

He frowned. "Well, maybe not."

"I sort of have a feeling it is. But if it helps for you to leave the possibility open, why not?"

"You know, one thing I've learned about you is that slender little streak of cynicism you've got."

"Well, who wants fat cynicism?"

He laughed. "You know what I mean."

"Accepted. You've told me that before, too."

"You mean I'm repeating myself? Probably we've both had too much to drink."

"No doubt. Webster would be shocked. Not to mention disappointed in us."

"No, he wouldn't. Webster would have been too busy chewing on his own guts."

"What a grotesque thought!"

He lifted his glass. "Right. I withdraw the statement. Here's to Webster."

"To Webster," she said, touching his glass with hers, "whoever or whatever he was."

He nodded, and then they both drank, already not thinking of Webster again.

BRUMBACHER BREATHING

It came to me indirectly, in the way of the most satisfying compliments, and I can still remember the warmth it radiated. Almost physical, like a bathtub filled with hot water sloshing gently as you step in—the mirror image of a small, hard, white boat in a choppy sea.

"Haycox does not suffer fools gladly." Seidlin recited this in the conference room, smiling obliquely, to my left, in the direction of Gordy. Of course, he was speaking of Brumbacher, who had just plodded out of the room, wading in galoshes.

"A thick little man with a big thick head," I'd mumbled as Brumbacher reached for the door.

"What?" Gordy, our president, asked, looking up over his spectacles.

"He's referring to our recently departed member," McDowell said.

"An offending member," I reminded them.

Gordy grinned out of one side of his mouth, scarcely grin enough to move a toothpick; but a grin, nonetheless.

And then Seidlin uttered his words to Gordy in a voice low enough that I might have been supposed not to hear: "Haycox does not suffer fools gladly."

"Nor gladly teach," I quoted awry; and Seidlin glanced at me sharply, a smile on my half of his mouth, while Gordy nodded and gave his attention back to the papers on the mirror-bright, polished surface of the vast walnut table before him.

Padded like a casket, the conference room swallowed the sounds of our voices without a gulp. Once I'd dreamed of it—all of us present, gathered in our customary places about the table—and we moved our mouths as if uttering words; but all was silent. Except for one noise: Brumbacher's heavy, labored exhalations, which we could feel on the backs of our hands (clasped identically, authoritatively over folder-clipped copies of the agenda) . . . the exhalations, alone, while the inhalations were as inaudible as our voices as we mutely conferred over our corporation's biweekly crises.

"He had to go to the bathroom," McDowell said, meaning Brumbacher, of course.

"The world is Brumbacher's bathroom," I said. Then, unable to leave it alone, said: "Bathrocker's Boomroom."

"Let's leave it alone," Gordy said severely, gathering his shoulders into high peaks, elbows on table, clasping his two hands together beneath his chin. It was his severe schoolmaster's posture—in itself a considerable invitation to ridicule.

"Note," I said, "that our president just referred to Brumbacher as *it*."

"Not true," Gordy corrected me. "I was referring to the issue, not the man. I suggest we drop *it*. And him."

"But before we do," McDowell said, "will somebody please explain to me why the son of a bitch is wearing those K Mart *galoshes?*"

"I picture him as *always* wearing galoshes, somehow," I mused. "Heavy footed; flapping, unbuckled."

"Perhaps his feet are cold," Gordy said, nodding speculatively, gravely. Brumbacher's galoshes flopping down the hallways being a fact requiring a more majestic explanation, perhaps; but cold feet were the only answer Gordy could come up with, so he compensated for its lack of dignity with an uncommonly dignified expression.

"I don't think he can lean over to pull them off," I said. "Or lift his feet. Choose one."

"I choose relevance to the issue at hand," Gordy said in his most pompous tone, looking above my head at some image of what he thought I should be. His hand rested upon the files relating to said issue.

"I can't understand what's come over the son of a bitch," Canelli said. Since Canelli was the quietest of us all, we unanimously paused to listen. "He keeps invading my space," Canelli went on. "Maybe it's the galoshes or something. Like he practically stands on my toes."

Gordy frowned. "I'll speak to him about those galoshes you are all so concerned about. And to be candid, there's some truth to your view; there's the corporate image, and all that. Clichés, no doubt, but true enough, all the same." He had gazed at me as he uttered these last words, viewing me as the *arbiter elegantiarum* in residence. No doubt.

"Let's admit that he's not what you'd call a graceful or sophisticated man," Campbell said, "and let it go at that."

"I personally don't like him breathing on my tie," I added, and everyone except Rowick laughed. Rowick was the only woman among us—first name, Theodora ("Teddi" to her friends, I'm told)—and she was next to Canelli in quietness. Then Campbell, McDowell, Seidlin, Gordy, and finally, myself. I was the talker, the wit, who did not (I'd just overheard and acknowledged to myself as an important, if not colossal, truth) suffer fools gladly.

Of course, I've omitted Brumbacher in the above list. But then, he didn't really belong among us at all. He was a startling anomaly, as anyone could plainly see. A toad among ferrets. However, if he *had* to be acknowledged and rated, he would probably fall somewhere between Seidlin and Gordy in frequency of comment. In total wordage (not at all the same thing), he would fall somewhat lower in his rating, as would I. McDowell, for instance, commented seldom, but spoke in long periods with exhaustive attention to detail and relentless reference to data.

Champion of the one-liners, I contributed little to total wordage; I was content to derail the obsessive conversational choo-choos of people like McDowell and Campbell (who had his own seizures of prolonged mauling of the obvious). Therefore, Brumbacher, sitting fat faced and vague behind thick glasses, breathing stertorously into whatever discussion obtained at the moment, was in a sense doing *my* thing: looking for openings for wry comment, or jostling the ponderously growing, elephantine subject off its tightrope into collapse. An essential role: without it, how could we ever start over, or— to begin with—finish?

But Brumbacher was chronically off without ever managing to be anything as interesting as offbeat. And he would have ranked even higher in frequency of comment, if he didn't have to go pee so often. He'd asked about this once, in this very room, facing us all at the table and wondering aloud if there was something wrong with him. It appears that somewhere at sometime he'd heard of diabetes.

What an opening! And my diagnoses would have ranged far from diabetes. Still, I managed to remain silent, even though my head rang with a fusillade of ripostes.

Because anybody could see there was a great deal wrong with him, and the only mystery was how anybody so relentlessly gauche, so loud and radiantly *stupid*, could have won a place at the great walnut table which Gordy presided over.

Someone had once said that Brumbacher had proved himself in Accounting, and that was why he'd been moved up into the inner circle. But I contested that, claiming that it was hard to believe that Brumbacher knew how to count at all, let alone function in our corporation with anything remotely similar to efficiency.

Hives of bees, it is said, have their own unique configurations, their own *gestalten;* individual bees are as cells in the total organism of the hive, so that you might even fancy that each hive is a unique personality.

From what perspective might we observe these peculiarities? Where might we stand so that we could perceive that this hive is an introvert, that hive a joker, and some third a potentially gifted concert pianist without hands?

Too fanciful, no doubt, but I sometimes wish that our corporation might achieve such integrity as a body. For example, how *actually* did someone like Brumbacher rise so high? I know I have already asked this question, but it continues to tease me. Suddenly, he was there among us, breathing audibly through his nose and trying his own hand at wit (in a manner of speaking, appropriate to the subject).

"Hey, Cox!" he shouted at me, relishing the play on words. "I thought you wrote westerns." Ernest Haycox, the once pop writer of westerns, you see: two witticisms in one sentence.

"What makes you think I don't?" I asked Brumbacher, returning the serve.

But there the volley ended. Brumbacher said: "You *do?*" And then laughed his way down the hallway, metaphorical galoshes flapping.

As for the actual galoshes: I do believe and confess that he was guilty of this only that one day (his *feet* being cold, as Gordy surmised; and his being afraid of the wetness of the world, too, no doubt).

The best explanation is political: Accounting had not had anyone rise to administration for six years, and Brumbacher was unaccountably chosen.

"Well," I said, "our loss is their gain."

In fact, I said this several times—once in front of Brumbacher himself. But he didn't—*actually* didn't—seem to get the point.

Accounting, indeed!

Of course, there was something wrong with him. Something deep, serious, irreversible: a leakage of personality, an embolus in the vessels necessary for what was once called social intercourse.

Devoid of anything approaching sensitivity, Brumbacher possessed his own little suite of offices—three, including his receptionist's and secretary's. Spanish oak desk: new, not approaching the venerable costliness of the walnut galleon we all sailed upon during our twice-weekly board meetings; silver-inset shaded mirrors, dark as funereal box frames, in the walls of the entranceway to his office; a window vast as a movie screen, overlooking the cloverleaf and river, with Unicord's enclave of buildings looming in gray eminence like great solid-state terminals on the other shore.

It was into this suite that Brumbacher came each morning. Walking toes out, he passed his receptionist—a young Danish woman with more taste in her left hand than Brumbacher could imagine—then passed his secretary, a prodigy of resourcefulness and tact, who could operate the office without anyone . . . but managed only with difficulty, given the grotesque fact of Brumbacher's authority. What did *he* have to do with such as these two splendid and knowledgeable women? What did he have to do with *us*?

I often thought of him sitting there oafishly, breathing through his mouth like an adenoidal boy, telling off-color stories into the telephone. Seidlin once theorized he really was trying to imitate *me*, and I answered that I had never in my life worn galoshes. "Well, there's more than that, of course," Seidlin muttered, winking one eye in speculation.

"Not with Brumbacher," I'd answered. "There *couldn't* be."

Gordy seemed incapable of perceiving the great, impressive, even majestic *nerdiness* of Brumbacher—a thought which paralyzed my faculties with regard to Gordy (a thin, stone-faced man with a conscience chiseled out of some fable by Nathaniel Hawthorne), until . . . until I realized that in Gordy's eyes, at least, Brumbacher was something of our corporation eccentric: basically solid, you understand, with sound judgment and morals. The latter, especially, being important to Gordy, whose first name, Nathan, had been passed down to him from some distant New England ancestor. Perhaps he even thought of Brumbacher as our corporation's version of a classic crazy English squire: Brumbacher as Erasmus Darwin, Jeremy Bentham, or Bertrand Russell. (The balloon of the imagination hisses, leaks, begins to spit gas, and falls to an earthen incredulity.)

McDowell mentioned one day that he'd heard Brumbacher's wife had left him. "Strange he ever found a woman to be with him long enough to leave him," I'd said.

McDowell frowned over his pipe and said, "Yes, there is that."

Which, it came to me later, was an utterly mysterious thing for McDowell to say; and I had no idea what he'd meant by it then, although it doesn't seem quite so mysterious now.

In the early grades of school, there is always a fat boy, breathing heavily, who crowds in front of you at the drinking fountain and at the same time manages to step on the arch of your foot. This boy is, of course, the gross, innocent, and inept creature you've grown out of and left behind.

He is also, unmistakably, Brumbacher. Your astonishment is so enormous and sudden, it keeps you from reacting. Until, that is, some second time, when you shove his fat shoulder so hard he moves to the side and looks up in dull surprise that you are there, and that you have shoved him back to where he should have been in the first place. He is wearing thick glasses, opaque as suet, and that may be one reason you don't hit him. But there is probably a deeper reason, compounded of something like a fear of one who is so unaware of prohibitions and taboos ("my living space," as Canelli said) that such matters seem not to exist for him.

One of the senior officers, Brumbacher evidently did not know how to spend money. He dressed like the owner and cook of a 1936 diner attending a funeral. I tried to remember what he'd dressed like in the old days, before his divorce and sudden rise in the corporation. (I picture his wife as pale and slender, yet a social ballast, so that when she stepped out of the gondola, Brumbacher's fat balloon rose swiftly.) Was it possible that he had dressed more or less decently back in Accounting, and had come to work without wearing galoshes, when he'd had a wife to tell him what to do and how to do it? Or was there something like defiance in his present clownishness?

I didn't know, couldn't remember. And the gross and insensitive Brumbacher that now beguiled and perplexed me eclipsed whatever dim memories I might have had of the sort of man he'd been back then. Having him crowd up to you and breathe on you made it difficult to think he'd ever been anything different.

"He invades *everybody's* space," I told them at the Thursday meeting, after Brumbacher had retired to pee.

Canelli, recognizing my reference to his, nodded, while Gordy frowned. Seidlin smiled at the ceiling, but said nothing.

When Brumbacher returned, I said: "Don't come a step closer. Stay right where you are, in your galoshes. You have become a monument for us, Brumbacher, and monuments never move."

Usually he managed something like a laugh at whatever I said, no matter how insulting. But this time, he ridiculously took it in, having heard, and said: "You don't think much of me, do you, Haycox?"

"I think of you a great deal of the time," I said. "Some would say too often and too much."

"That isn't what I meant," Brumbacher said heavily, "and I think you know it."

"I think he does too," Seidlin muttered, and everyone at the table laughed.

Which proved to be our last laugh at Brumbacher's expense, because he died of a coronary in his sleep that night, and the next morning I heard of the trouble his secretary was having raiding the files, trying to find a current address for his ex-wife, so she could be properly notified.

Of course, our attendance at Brumbacher's funeral was obligatory. Although, as I told Seidlin, Brumbacher himself would be the last to understand such an obligation.

Seidlin was oddly unresponsive, off balance. Gordy did not look at me, but then, why should he have? Except for the fact that I almost stepped on his feet as I worked my way, steaming vapors of Scotch, toward the only vacant seat, embarrassingly near the front. I had, in fact, stepped on the soles of his shoe without touching the foot part. I felt the ridge quickly pulled back under the edge of my own shoe, and whispered an apology.

I was a little drunk, but nothing could have prevented my realizing that this was one of the worst funeral sermons (a class of rituals characterized, if not identified, by relentless mediocrity) I had ever heard. I found myself wondering if the minister had somehow known Brumbacher: he *sounded* like someone who had known him.

And yet, there was nothing festive here, and I'm relieved that this was so. I might have fallen for it and proved the worst offender. Because there were proprieties, after all, and even (as I thought then) Brumbacher should not have the power to break their seal.

Viewing the corpse, I could not help wondering if there were galoshes on its feet, safely hidden under the closed part of the casket.

This feverish humor was too obscene to be shared with anyone, of course; so I settled down with my coat in my lap (why hadn't I taken it off and hung it in the vestibule closet?) and gazed at the tip of my shoe as it bounced lightly from my pulse.

Brumbacher dead. An empty chair at the conference table, between McDowell and Rowick. Teddi Rowick was there, looking handsome and pretty in black; and somebody said that Brumbacher's wife was there, too; but I didn't ask which one she was, because I didn't want to know. There are some things best left untouched, after all.

The day was cold and sunny, and as I was about to step outside the funeral home, into the intermediary darkness of the awning-shaded portico, I heard a man's voice say: "Had he been sick at all? Does anybody know? Or was it just, you know, all of a sudden?"

"Not all of a sudden," I muttered to myself; and at that moment, as if receiving fresh and astonishing information from my own voice, I stopped and swayed a little on my feet.

Even then, I thought. *That's what he was doing.*

"What?" I heard myself ask, standing there under the awning as the hearse moved up.

But before I could answer this question, an attendant—a sleek, fat young man with curled sideburns and a long upper lip—came up to me and said: "Mr. Haycox, are you ready?"

I looked at him.

"You are one of the pallbearers, aren't you?" he asked.

I nodded, then let myself be eased into position so that I could help ease the casket into the hearse.

Later, I wondered why someone hadn't bothered to introduce me to the widow, but then it occurred to me that everything was done without direction, except from those professionals at the funeral home. How could they have chosen me as one of the pallbearers upon any basis other than the fact that Brumbacher and I sat at the same conference table twice a week? Could Gordy have given my name? I think it would have been sardonic of him.

But this was not important, and even when I was musing upon it, I realized that it was not.

That evening, I told my wife that I would not miss Brumbacher.

"What an odd thing to say!" she answered. "Whoever would have supposed you would?"

We were having drinks before our open fire. It was a cozy scene, for the cold sunshine of morning had turned into a sullen, cold, dark winter evening. "An evening fit for galoshes," I said to my wife, and she said: "Please, don't start on that again."

I shook my head. "No, there'll be no reason for it now."

"None whatsoever."

"The poor contemptible son of a bitch."

"Please don't," my wife said.

Then we sat and thought our own private thoughts for a while, sipping our drinks. And it was then that I began to feel something like dismay and fear come crowding in. It was as secret and intimate as breathing, only it was just myself, or part of myself, returning from some distant place.

"What is it?" my wife asked, no doubt seeing an expression of something or other on my face.

I sloshed my drink and narrowed my eyes. "Don't ever mock a fool," I said.

"I have no intention of doing so," she answered; and I believed her. But then, I wasn't addressing her, anyway.

"You do feel bad about him, don't you?" she said, reaching over and touching my wrist with her fingers.

"Not exactly *bad*," I said, frowning over the problem. "Maybe perplexed. I should have known, you know."

"Known what?"

"That this perspective is always waiting, always possible. It's with us all the time."

"What is?"

"The mirror image. The eventual hole we'll leave."

"I don't like it when you get morbid."

"Nor do I."

"Then, cheer up, why don't you?"

"You didn't let me finish."

"Well, finish, then, so it will be over with."

"I'll finish, but it won't be over with."

She shook her head rapidly and leaned over to gaze into my eyes. "All right, dearest," she said. "What was it you were going to say?"

"I can still hear him breathing."

"Oh, stop it!"

"Stertorous breathing can be a cardiac symptom, you know."

"Sometimes," she said, nodding. "Yes."

"He was dying slowly, deliberately, relentlessly. Even when he came up from Accounting."

"That is too melodramatic and silly, and you know it."

"Only true."

"Farfetched and an extremely remote possibility, if possible at all."

"I think it was literally true. He was dying while invading our space. The fact that he might have been the last person in the world to know about it only emphasizes its truth. But then, such might not be a fact, after all. Might. Might."

"Exactly. And isn't that enough?"

I thought about that a moment, and then, almost like a man quoting, said: "Don't ever mock a fool, because a fool's death is unanswerable."

For a long while she thought about that. Then she nodded and said, "They do become something different, don't they?"

"We all do."

"Of course," my wife said, "but then, that isn't the point after all, is it?"

Naturally, she was right, and I told her so, in order that she might share a little of the guilt and sadness I felt at this moment for a person who had never, really, existed at all, so far as I could tell.

Designed by Glen Burris
Set in Baskerville text and Light Roman display
by Blue Heron
Printed on 50-lb. Sebago Eggshell Cream
by The Maple Press Company, Inc.